HUNTED

**Stories of death and disaster,
of triumph and victory –
ever remembering
the hunter's fearsome traps**

I0682885

Edited by Dorothy Davies

HUNTED

GRAVESTONE PRESS

CONTENTS

In the Gloaming

Rie Sheridan Rose

Sadie glanced uneasily around the clearing. She'd lost track of the time and started for home much later than she'd intended. The path she walked was as familiar as her face in the mirror, but she usually didn't venture through the wood at night.

She took a deep breath—filling her lungs with the smell of cedar and damp earth. It had rained earlier, which was one reason she hadn't started home at her usual time. That and the bliss of being with the friends she hadn't seen in ages. Marty, Ben, Amanda... how she had missed them.

Thoughts of the meet-up momentarily had distracted her, but her focus came back with laser-like strength and swiftness as she heard a noise behind her on the trail. A sharp crack, like someone had stepped on a twig.

She gulped, and forced herself forward. It was time to be home, safe behind walls and locked doors. The news had been full of reports of a new killer on the loose. No one knew where he would strike next, or how. He had no real pattern, but still—perhaps because the alternative was too awful to contemplate—the police were sure that all the recent murders were the work of the same perpetrator.

He would lure his victim somewhere isolated... like this path. At a time when there were no witnesses... like twilight. And do whatever dastardly deed he had chosen for this particular victim's fate.

She shivered. So random. How could one plan a defense for someone like that?

She heard another twig snap and a low whistling behind her.

She picked up the pace and hurried across the clearing. She was soon deeper in the cover of the wood. She could always step off the path and hide if necessary.

The whistling grew louder and she heard footsteps now—measured, unhurried, someone confident in his or her own safety. Must be nice.

Visibility was narrowing as the gloaming deepened. It would be too dark to see soon. The air had that shade between violet and purple that she never could remember, and the crickets were starting to tune up for their nightly concert.

The footsteps were quickening behind her. Her skin prickled into goosebumps as another shiver ran through her. The air was cooling as well. She couldn't run in this light, it was asking for a twisted ankle. What could she do?

The trees seemed to press closer, urging her down the path. If she recalled, correctly, there was another small clearing just ahead...

She began speeding up as much as she dared, then hurried across the clearing and ducked behind a broken tree stump. Heart pounding in her chest, she waited.

The man who entered the clearing behind her was medium-height and thin to the point of emaciation. His clothes were torn and she could smell the body odor despite the space between them.

Sadie smiled lazily. Indigent, most likely. The sort who were seldom missed. It was a bonus that she'd been late leaving the meet-up. She might have missed this chance.

She slipped her hand into her pocket. She brought it out, clutching a switchblade.

This one should be fun.

A Taste of Hunter's Meat

David Turnbull

Me and Henry were sitting on the lip of a bomb crater, tossing stones into the muddy brown water pooled in its belly. Henry was munching on a sausage roll his mum had wrapped in waxed paper.

"Want a bite?" he asked.

"What's in it?"

Henry chuckled. "Don't play dumb, Ron. You know exactly what's in it. That old tart we found in that garden on Turpin Lane."

I shook my head.

"I'll pass."

Henry held out the sausage roll.

"Go on. You know you want to."

He was right. The curiosity had been nagging at me for days. A wicked little thrill buzzed through me as I closed my hand around the sausage roll. What did the meat inside it actually taste like? How would it feel to swallow it down?

I thought of the woman we'd found in the garden of the burning house, all bomb black and blistered, skirts up to her knickers. That made me hesitate. It was one thing folk buying produce from Henry's parents' shop. They were mostly oblivious to what they were eating. But if you knew. For example, if you knew the meat in a sausage roll came from an old tart you found in a garden in

Turpin Lane. If you knew that and you still ate it. That was different. That made you a cannibal.

"Why does your old man call it hunter's meat?" I asked.

"He reckons what we're doing is like hunters in the old days. We're bringing meat back to the village so the tribe can survive the winter."

"It's still summer."

"I think he's using *winter* as a metaphor for the war," said Henry.

"Go on." He'd noticed my pained procrastination. "Every hunter deserves a taste of the meat he brought home."

Here goes nothing, I thought, squeezing my eyes shut and chomping down.

The pastry was flaky. The 'meat' succulent and well-seasoned. I didn't gag as I had been worried I might. I enjoyed it so much I was taking a second bite before I even realised.

"Finish it," said Henry. "Then we can go a get a whole one from my mum for you to eat later."

***

That night we were out on the streets long before the all clear sounded. The sky was dark and moonless. We could still hear the drone of German bombers prowling above. There came a distant thump and roar. The ground juddered as another bomb hit the docks.

Like scavenging rats, we moved swiftly through the gloom, weaving around heaps of rubble and clambering over fallen masonry. Swirls smoke drifted about us like ghostly dancers. It made our eyes stream. We had to cover our faces with neckerchiefs to stop us from coughing up our guts.

But we were quick and proficient. We'd done this so often now we had it down to a tee. The trick was to find a corpse that wasn't buried under too much rubble. That way we could be off with it without getting nobbled by the wardens.

The kid we came across wasn't much older than us. Fourteen or fifteen, I'd say. He was sprawled on his back amongst the shattered glass and splintered wood of a blown-out window frame. Blood was oozing sluggishly from a big gash on his head. He hadn't been long dead.

"Blimey O'Reilly," said Smiffy, once we'd brushed the dust from his face. "He looks the spit of Nora Wilson's cousin."

I leaned closer for a better look. "He is Nora Wilson's cousin!"

"Blimey O'Reilly," said Smiffy again.

"We should leave him," said Del. "See if we can find a different one."

"Meat is meat," insisted Henry. "Cousin or no bleedin' cousin. Let's get him in the wheelbarrow and scarper before we're rumbled."

No sooner had we gotten the wheelbarrow into the back room of Henry's dad's shop than the siren wailed for the all clear. We lifted the cadaver onto the slab and began to strip it naked. There was big bin where we put all the shoes and clothes so they could be donated to the Salvation Army.

Henry's dad appeared, tying the strings around his striped butcher's apron.

"What have you got for me tonight, lads?" he asked.

"Young 'un, mister Dunn.' I said.

He came and pinched the kid's cold flesh between his finger and thumb.

"A bit scrawny but I reckon he'll mince up nicely."

Henry brought him a candle and some matches. Once the candle was lit, he began burning away all the hairs on the kid's body. The air hung heavy with the acrid reek of the singeing. It was ten time worse that the smoke we'd encountered outside.

While he was using the hot candle wax to pluck up all the residual bristles Smiffy and Del went to the outside tap and filled up a couple of buckets of soapy water. Henry's dad fetched his bone saw. I turned to one side. By then we'd brought Henry's dad dozens of corpses but the removal of the head was the bit that always sickened me. The sound of the saw's teeth grinding against the neck bones gave me the chills.

"Give us an 'and, Ron," said Henry, when the job was done.

When I turned, the kid's severed head was already sitting upright on one of Mr Dunn's chopping blocks. Henry popped open the mouth and I crammed it full of little silver ball bearings to give it more weight. Mr Dunn wrapped the head up in brown paper and tied it with string. Then Henry dropped it into a sack. The first chance we got we'd toss it into the canal. There had to be at least thirty heads down there by then, gathering silt amongst the rusted bicycle frames and other junk.

While all this was going on, Smiffy and Del had been washing the cadaver, cleaning away the blood and grime and stray curls of burned pubic hair, then scrubbing it thoroughly with a scouring brush. Mr Dunn took a rope and tied it around the corpse's ankles. Then he hefted up onto the gurney to let it bleed out from the neck.

"Line up, lads," he said, standing back, hands on hips, to look at the freshly scrubbed pink body. "Time to settle up." The four of us lined up before him. We were grinning from ear to ear as he dropped a thruppenny bit into each of our palms.

***

According to Henry it all started by a complete fluke.

One night he and his parents had been to the Empire to see the latest George Formby flick. They were walking back, chuckling about George's antics, when up ahead this drunk old geezer got hit on the bonce from a dislodged brick which fell from a bombed-out terrace house.

Their butcher shop was nearby. So, they helped him to his feet and took him there and sat him in a chair behind the counter. Henry went to fetch him glass of water, while Mrs Dunn tended to the huge bump that was swelling up something rotten on his forehead.

Just when it seemed as if he was going to be right as rain, he lets out a groan, clutches his chest and pegs it from a heart attack right there in the chair. He slumps to left and Mr Dunn has to grab him so as to stop him collapsing onto the floor.

"Well, this is inconvenient," complains Henry's dad.

"Should I go find a copper?" asks Henry.

Before Henry's dad can reply, Henry's mum pipes up.

"We're low on stock," she goes. "Not many pig carcasses getting delivered to Smithfield. It would be a shame to let all this meat go to waste."

"We couldn't," goes Henry's dad.

"Who's to stop us?" goes Henry's mum. "Who's to know?"

They all looked at each other and, the way Henry put it, they agreed the whole thing without actually uttering another word.

"Go fetch my bone saw," goes Henry's dad.

Henry fetches the bone saw.

I suppose from then on the Dunns became what could be called profiteers. The war presented them with an opportunity and they enthusiastically seized it. The *rationale of rationing* is what Mr Dunn started calling it. If you can supply more of something that is in short supply, then it stands to reason that you're going to come out on top.

Word got out that you got more meat for your ration coupons at Dunn's the Butcher. There was plenty of mince to be had. As well as liver, kidney, heart and tripe. So fresh it was almost steaming. People queued along the street.

By the time Henry had enlisted our support in retrieving cadavers, the Dunns had branched out and acquired a pie and mash shop that everyone thought would be closed for the duration. It was like Sweeny bleedin' Todd all over again.

If the authorities had gotten wind of any of it the Dunns would have been for the hangman's noose. The rest of us would likely have gone down for life. But Mr Dunn had taken precautions. He had the local beat bobby in his pocket. A pound of mince and a rack of ribs every Friday was enough to keep him from asking questions and poking his nose where it wasn't welcome.

As a backup measure, Mr Dunn had also enlisted the support of our neighbourhood gangsters. I say gangsters. But they weren't gangsters like you used to see in the Jimmy Cagney or Edward G Robinson flicks. They were just half a dozen sixteen year olds from the tenements who weren't quite old enough to be conscripted. If the real hard men had still been around, they'd have been slapped into place pronto. But with no one to maintain that sort of pecking order, they kind of ruled the roost.

Henry said they knew exactly where his dad sourced his meat supplies and that their cut for protection was a big pot of hands and feet that Henry's mum would boil up for them with carrots and onions, just like pig's trotters. Henry said that they boasted that they were getting practice in for when they got called up. They said they couldn't wait for the day they got to chop off some Nazi hands and gnaw on them for supper.

***

A couple of days after we'd found Nora Wilson's cousin, we saw Nora stuffing her face in the pie and mash shop. "Your old ma makes delicious pies," she said to Henry, talking over a mouth crammed with meat and pastry.

"You look like you're enjoying it," said Del.

"I always eat loads when I'm upset," said Nora.

"What's upset you?" I asked, acting all innocent.

"My cousin William 's been missing since the last air raid," she said, shovelling more of the meaty pie into her mouth.

"He may be much closer than you think," said Henry, turning and winking at us.

"It does feel like that," sighed Nora, wiping away some gravy dribbling down her chin.

"Blimey O'Reilly," said Smiffy. "Careful some of 'im doesn't spill on your blouse."

Nora swallowed down the content of her mouth.

"What that supposed to mean?" she asked.

Smiffy blushed and gave her a panicky response. "I meant 'it'. Don't let some of 'it' spill on your blouse. The gravy. Careful none of the gravy spills on your blouse."

"Where did you last see him?" I asked her, swiftly changing the subject.

Nora shrugged. "He came for dinner at my mum's. We had sausages from Henry's dad's shop." She mopped up the gravy on her plate with a slice of bread. "This is so bloody good I might order a second helping."

The way she said it reminded me of that first time I had partaken in hunter's *'meat'*. I wondered who had been in the sausages Nora and her mum had eaten with her poor departed cousin. I wondered if the sausages were still in his system when Henry's dad did the butchering of his headless corpse.

***

At some point a murder was almost inevitable.

It happened one night when the Luftwaffe had been particularly busy. It was like we were running through hell, roaring fires and collapsing buildings at every turn. I could feel the heat blistering my skin and the smoke searing my lungs.

Luckily we found a corpse relatively quickly.

The geezer we found had only one leg. Which was probably why he hadn't reached the air raid shelter in time. His crutches were splintered and broken from the bomb blast that had felled him. Henry said it meant less meat for his dad to mince, but none of us wanted to be out there any longer than we had to. We insisted that, one leg or not, *he* had to be the one.

He was half covered in a big heap of ash and dirt. Having recently acquired a shovel, we had him out and into the wheelbarrow in jiffy. We were rushing back to Mr Dunn's shop when an ARP warden with a big white W painted on his helmet stepped out and blocked our way.

"What have we got here then?" he demanded. "A bunch of filthy looters, I'll bet."

"You've got us wrong," I said, rapidly constructing a lie. "We found this bloke in the rubble. We was taking him to get help."

The warden looked at the one-legged body in the wheelbarrow.

"Leg got blown clean off," said Del.

"I'll fetch someone," said the warden, raising his tin whistle to his lips.

Before he could blow on it, Henry whacked him hard with the shovel. His knees crumpled under his weight as he fell to the ground. His helmet clattered away onto the road. Henry stepped up and whacked him again and cracked open his exposed skull.

"What did you go and to that for?" demanded Del.

"He was going to blow his whistle," said Henry. "Cops would have come running from every bleedin' corner."

"They'd have believed our story," I said. "I'm mean, how was we to know the geezer would peg it after we put him in the wheelbarrow?"

"And how would we have accounted for being out in the middle of an air raid with wheelbarrow and shovel?" asked Henry. "We'd still have been taken for looters. And then they'd have started asking questions. One of us could easily have cracked under the pressure."

"Blimey O'Reilly," said Smiffy. "What are we going to do now?"

"Meat is meat," said Henry.

"We'll need to strip him down to his underwear then," I said.

"Why?" asked Del.

"We can't go giving away an ARP uniform to the Sally Army," I said. "We'd have avoided one set of questions only to invite a whole lot more."

We hurried to remove the uniform and tossed it, along with the helmet, into the nearest house fire. It was hard going pushing two corpses in the wheelbarrow, even if one of them had a leg missing. But we made it before the all clear sounded. Mr Dunn was so chuffed with our haul that we all got a tanner each that night, instead of a thruppenny bit.

***

"I can't believe we did a murder," said Smiffy.

"Well to be exact," said Del, "it was Henry what did the murder. We was just accessories after the fact."

"No one will ever know," said Henry. "As long as we all keep it zipped."

"Loose talk costs lives," agreed Smiffy.

We were sitting on the patchy grass on the bank of the canal. Two more heads, weighed down with ball bearings, were sinking to the bottom. Henry's mum had made another batch of sausage rolls. We had one each, wrapped in waxed paper. They were fresh out of the oven and still warm.

I took a big bite out of mine and chowed down. I didn't know if I was eating the warden or the one-legged man. Either way the meat was delicious. It filled the hollow space that had been echoing all morning in my belly.

"Sooner or later the war will be over," I said, once I'd swallowed.

"Then we can stop collecting corpses," said Smiffy. "There won't be any more rationing. Things can go back to normal."

"That's assuming we win," I said.

"Of course we'll win," insisted Del.

Smiffy finished his sausage roll and stood up to skim a stone across the water.

"Remember Dunkirk," I said. "We're not guaranteed to win."

"Traitor," said Del.

"Just pointing out that we should prepare for any eventuality," I replied.

"Blimey O'Reilly," said Smiffy, skimming another stone. "If the Gerries cross the Channel there could be jackboots goosestepping down Bethnal Green."

"If we lose, we have to swear to carry on," said Henry. "It'll be our patriotic duty to kill Nazis and butcher them for food."

"What if we could kill Hitler?" said Smiffy.

"We could send Churchill a dozen Adolf sausages," said Del.

"Or Hitler's head wrapped up in brown paper," said Henry.

We all laughed.

**

We became real hunters after that night.

Henry did all of the killing, armed with one of his dad's boning knives. Me, Del and Smiffy had

21

the job of herding the victims. We'd go out as soon as the air raid siren started sounding and corral our selected victim into a dark alley with promises of a quick shortcut to the nearest shelter.

By the time we were half way into the darkness, Henry would pounce and slit them from groin to rib cage. I ran off to fetch the wheelbarrow from wherever we'd hidden it. Meanwhile Del and Smiffy would drag the body to the nearest gutter and spill the guts into the drain.

It was all pretty efficient. Safer too. We were usually back at Henry's dad's place before the bombs started falling. What's more, Henry's dad was so chuffed with our productivity that he upped our pay rate to a shilling a corpse.

One night we did a sailor down near Deptford. His wallet fell open on the pavement when Del and Smiffy were dragging his corpse toward the gutter. There was a crumpled photograph inside. "Blimey O'Reilly," said Smiffy, seeing the young girl and boy posing for a family snap. "This poor geezer survived the North Atlantic. But now he'll never go back home because of us."

"Meat is meat," insisted Henry.

"It's not," said Smiffy. "Meat is people. And we've got blood on our hands."

"I don't hear you complaining when my old man puts a shilling in your bloody hand," said Henry.

"We're hunters," said Del. "We're bringing meat back to the village, that's all."

Smiffy started crying.

"We're not hunters. We're monsters. We're going to burn in hell for what we've done."

I looked at the murdered sailor, bleeding like a gutted fish from the gash in his belly. All I could think of was all the sausage rolls I'd eaten since that first taste by the bomb crater. Suddenly I was staggering back into the alley and puking up all over the wall.

**

Obviously, history confirms there were no jackboots goose-stepping down Bethnal Green.

Instead there was a carnival on the 8th of May 1945. We danced in the fountains in Trafalgar Square and congaed through Piccadilly. We had our first taste of beer. We were relieved in more way than one.

It was over.

It was all over.

About a week after VE Day the Dunns did a bunk. The butcher's and the pie and mash shop were locked up, shutters down. We looked through the windows of their terraced house. All the furniture was gone.

We surmised they'd figured that with the war over someone would let something slip and the lid would be blown on what they'd been up to. They needn't have worried. No one was about to grass, or even inadvertently mention what had gone on.

All of the sixteen year olds who'd been in that little gang had ended up dead on the beaches of Normandy. I guess they never got the chance to gnaw down on a Nazi knuckle. For my money, one of them would have been most likely to blow the lid.

No one else was talking.

A subdued mood descended over the neighbourhood. People walked with their heads down, not making eye contact with one another, consumed it seemed by a deeply introverted guilt. It appeared what everyone had been supplementing their rations with was common knowledge and nowhere near as big a secret as we'd all assumed.

It hit me bad. I vomited constantly for three consecutive days. My dad, who had been demobbed by then, told my mum that they should call out a doctor. My mum said I would be fine once I got it out of my system. When our eyes met, I knew for sure that she knew what I knew.

Without Henry to anchor us ,Del, Smiffy and me gradually drifted apart.

To start with we'd walk school in dreary silence, afraid of what horrible truths a conversation might lead to. At school we'd avoid each other. After school we'd hang around with different crowds. It didn't take too long before we became total strangers.

A few years later Del contracted malaria while on national service in Malaysia. He died out there when it developed into pneumonia. I heard Smiffy emigrated to Australia. Every now and then I have a little chuckle to myself thinking about him exclaiming 'Blimey O'Reilly' in an Aussie accent.

I never heard anything more about Henry Dunn and his parents.

I may well be the last man standing.

Over the years I somehow subconsciously suppressed the memory of the terrible things we'd done during the blitz. Flushed them completely out of my head. Never thought about it, certainly never talked about it. It wasn't till many years afterwards, in the bleak gulf of grief and loneliness that flooded the aftermath of my wife's passing that I recalled what Nora Wilson had said that day in the pie and mash shop about how she always ate when she was upset.

A good hot meal was exactly what I needed. But there wasn't much in the cupboards at home. Austerity and benefit cuts were at their height. Without the wife's pension to supplement the household income I'd been struggling to make ends meet, relying on the generosity of the local foodbank. It was like rationing all over again.

I was crouching down to open the fridge door when the recollection of Nora's words triggered a series luridly vivid flashbacks of the Dunns and all the gruesome details of what had transpired. I remembered that first sausage roll. Me and Henry sitting on the lip of that bomb crater. How delicious it had seemed. My mouth began to salivate in an oddly nostalgic manner that both appalled and invigorated me.

I started almost instantaneously to crave the taste of hunter's meat.

I tried desperately to fight it and failed miserably.

I considered all the pensioners, benefit claimants and single mothers I'd met at the foodbank. It was like the war all over again. Different time, different enemy. But those on high were dropping bombs on us that were just as devastating as those that blitzed London all those years ago.

I found myself absently smacking my lips. Appalling as it may seem, there was only one thing that would fix me. Once I was strong enough, I would fix everyone else. I'd be a hunter once more. I'd bring back enough meat to my village to see my tribe through the hard winter that had descended on us. I'd be a ghoulish Robin Hood, slaughtering the rich to feed the poor.

I put on my overcoat, my cap and scarf. Took a large knife from the kitchen drawer. Made my way down the graffiti adorned stairwell. Went out into the night. Headed to the newly gentrified area down by the train station. *Teach them to goosestep all over my turf,* I muttered as I went.

Black Metal in a White Room

SJ Townend

"Mr Monkton? Answer the door. The door."

I hadn't wanted to answer the door. At all. I knew full well who it'd be: one of the Empties, collecting. No-one else had the nerve to bang on so hard and so fast for so damn long.

"We're after one pint today. One pint."

They'd been rude and insistent ever since they'd taken over. I detested the way they spoke too, echoing everything, cacophonous enough without the additional reverb. Their voices hurt. Their words ricocheted in the air like orchestral gunfire, like shards of glass, like black metal. And I am not a black metal fan. I like classic rock. But I didn't dare say anything, ask them to drop their volume—the Empties were not beings to be messed with and they sure as heck didn't handle requests with pleasantries.

"Yeah, sure. I know. I'm coming," I said. I switched off my screen, grabbed my bag and shut my front door behind me on my way out.

***

Everything changed the day the Empties came to Earth. No-one really knew what they were or where they'd come from, but they weren't looking for friendship, or seeking to embrace our culture, that was for certain. The newsreaders said they'd *'slid down a moonbow'* in the middle of the night. No-one had seen them arrive *per se*—due to their invisibility—but many claimed to have seen their ominous shadows bounding down from the night sky under lunar light.

We couldn't see them, but we could always hear them. Everyone heard them alright, with their distorted foghorn sounds and their ear-splitting wah-wah voices and their tone of Cradle of Filth. The racket they made was the opposite of music to the ear, enough to make your windows rattle, your molars hum.

***

He or it or whatever it was that'd disturbed my gaming session by knocking on my door that cloudy morning led me to the train station once more. I tagged along behind it, a knot of apprehension making a pretzel of my innards, all the while trying to avoid placing my foot directly on all I could see of it, its trailing shadow of black static. I was distracted by a feral cat darting from behind a bin and my toe fell within the hazy prickles its presence scattered on the pavement. The thing—the 'Empty'—let out a blood-curdling scream. I apologised profusely, fear bubbled beneath my skin and I stepped with caution as if walking on egg shells for the remainder of the journey. I knew full well I'd be of no use to them with curdled blood.

It was taking me to make a transaction. Each payment journey to the old church hall in the next district anyone made was always chaperoned, despite the escorting being totally unnecessary. We all had a damn good idea about what happened to people who *didn't* obey and it wasn't pretty, yet still, each week, a knock at the door would pull me away from my VR screen and a satanic shadow would be hovering over my coir doormat, waiting to take me away.

At least it felt pleasant to be outside for a while, away from the four ever-pressing walls of my own front room where I'd been cooped up since the Empties arrived. A moment of weak, autumnal sunshine broke through the cloud, hit me on my cheek, gave me a little hope. A little vitamin D stirred in my cells.

***

As far as I could gather, all the Empties were cruel, but some of them were rogue and took more than just the odd donation. People had been going missing. Society had broken down; most people had decided to stay in, watch mindless television shows or joined the virtual reality gaming realm, all existing on the just-about-adequate provisions our uninvited guests trundled about not quite regularly enough (I'd had to make an extra hole in my belt.). We had the internet to communicate with though: chat rooms, email, face-time and so on, but for those of us without close family or friends, existence was paramount to isolation.

My VR escape stage—*Classic Rock Concert Pro*—had become the main source of joy in my life.

I definitely wasn't happy, what with the apocalyptic invasion going on the other side of my black curtains, but at least I had entertainment to help pass the time. An innate urge to survive powered me onwards each day. We were all hopeful things would get better.

I hopped on the train, nodded across the carriage at another man sitting under the veil of a doom-shadow. Poor guy was probably heading to the same place I was. Too tired to make conversation—the payment I'd made last week had knocked the stuffing out of me—I simply raised my eyebrows and nodded at him, a gesture which he, looking equally as exhausted, returned. I rubbed my sore arms and contemplated asking the Empty escorting me if it'd be possible to make my prospective payment from a vessel in my leg instead this time. I had more track marks than a heroin addict and some of them looked infected. I decided against asking it whilst sat on the train—I'd wait until I arrived at the payment centre. This decision was partly due to my lethargy and partly because I didn't want to inflict the sound of its horrible, shuddering, thrashing voice on the chap sat opposite me. Not unless I had to.

***

An hour later, the shadow wrapped me up with a roar and shoved me through the door of the payment centre. I rolled up the length of my trouser, pointed to the back of my knee.

"Any chance we could take it from here today," I said and placed my fingers in my ear drums. The hideous noise from its invisible gob thundered out, a chill skittered down my spine.

"Yes. Yes. If we can find a vein. A vein."

I felt a revolting pressure, the tangible equivalent of a fork scraping down a blackboard, a guitar string snapping, as the Empty pushed me back and groped and shuffled its invisible parts all over my body, searching for a suitable blood vessel.

I have no idea which part of its body it used to jam the needle into my groin but it did so with the bedside manner of Dr. Harold Shipman. The sharp steel spike entered my skin and the vein beneath it, causing me to let out a yelp. Red stuttered out at first in dribs and drabs and then gushed down the plastic tubing, eager to escape. It filled up the bag on the end of the line which appeared to be floating in front of me, suspended somehow by the invisible, rough-handed monster. As my blood collected, the Empty jabbed another needle—this one attached to a syringe-full of black static—into my thigh. "In exchange, exchange," it hollered. I dug my grubby fingernails into the palms of my balled fists, channelling the sharp pain through and out of my limbs. Dang. What the heck was being pumped into my body in exchange for my blood?

I was left to pull the canula needles dangling from my groin out myself once my blood had filled the pint sack. It had what it wanted. It immediately lost interest in my de-juiced body.

***

31

How long would a pint take to replenish? The internet told me it'd take 48 hours to top up the volume of liquid I'd lost, a further 4 to 8 weeks to manufacture and replace the red blood cells. This was my seventh payment. They'd come every week, like clockwork, to march me to the donation centre, to drain me like the dregs from an upturned bottle of Merlot. No wonder I felt like death warmed up.

On my way out, I glanced back to see the bag of my blood arc through the air—a crimson-sailed boat bobbing along unseen wave crests—until it stopped in the corner. There, it was tipped up, emptied, into what I can only presume was the feeding organ of an Empty. I watched the red dripping down, shifting, glugging, becoming momentarily an out-of-focus polygon of sorts. The vermillion shape throbbed in time with my own heart beat as if the liquid were still present within my viscera. Then the air-puddle faded away to nothing and the bag dropped like a stone.

Were the bastards drinking it? A crisp burp—oddly echoless this time, a violent duck-quack—came from the corner above the emptied blood bag which lay discarded on the floor.

Disgusting.

Whatever these invisi-beasts were, they had appalling table manners. The belch was followed by a series of smaller burps and a satanic shriek of a giggle. The sound ripples hit my eardrums. A wave of vomit thrummed against the walls of my oesophagus, eager to escape my fragile body—as eager as I was to get the heck away from the slovenly, blood-drinking toads.

I was dizzy with blood loss, so legged it back to the station and caught a train back home.

At least the payment covered me for another week. A pint a week—that seemed to be the going rate for internet. A pint for internet, a half for electricity and a half for food, water, the essentials. It was rough, but manageable. After making a payment, rehydration was key and maybe a couple of biscuits, then back I went, into my virtual reality game. I was okay with a pint each week.

They'll get bored, I thought, they'll go home soon.

Things'll get better. Life'll return to normal.

***

The next day, the familiar, excessive knock at my front door came again—albeit a little earlier than I'd anticipated. A whole six days earlier. I was mid-performance.

I paused my game, inhaled deeply and admired the faux view. Jack Bruce stood to my left. He repetitively shifted from side to side, his bass guitar hiccupped in and out of virtual existence, his microphone stand flickered on, off, on, off. I glanced behind me—Ginger Baker, head tipped back, a pair of drumsticks hung blurred in the air in front of him mid-paradiddle. I lifted my foot from the special effects pedal, slung my Gibson Les Paul behind me and waved goodbye to my incandescent, glitching audience of thousands. The sound of the unholy transparent beast knocking and screaming at my front door had drowned out the song anyway.

I pulled my nose away from the centre of the large wall-mounted screen and the device *switched-off*—the blank canvas hung, desolate on the wall of my otherwise sparse living room; a rectangular body draped from the gallows of my white wall.

I'd been centre stage at Wembley arena from the comfort of my own living room but the knocking and screaming had grown more persistent.

I grumbled to no-one and yanked my body up from the couch. The puncture wound in my puce groin oozing a translucent yellow pus which dripped down my inner thigh like sour tears from heaven. I still ached heavily from the abuse endured the day before. They must've made a mistake knocking for me again so soon.

I fumbled for my bag and coat and caught sight of myself in the reflective black screen; a walking disaster. Drawn cheeks, waxen skin pale as my white walls, under-eye bags dark and inky as my black curtains. I must've lost ten kilos since the arrival of the Empties. Loose skin hung, almost dripping from my slouched frame.

It knocked again with its dreadful hand of nothingness. "I'm coming," I shouted.

I answered the door. Dirty shadows scuttled on the floor by where I imagined its feet might be— or the base of its hexagon or polygon or tesseract or whatever the heck its true form was. A cloak was draped over its rippling nothingness. Akin to some kind of horrific Emperor's New Clothes role-reversal parody, a black, hooded cape was suspended over my door step, a menacing shadow flitting about beneath.

"Hurry. Hurry," it said. Its voice shook dust from my windowsill, filled my boots with dread.

"I made a payment yesterday," I quivered.

"Rate increase. Increase. Increase," it replied with extra distortion. I wanted to ask why, why me, why again, why more blood? But I needed its thunderous, searing voice to stop.

I marched behind it to the station, hopped dejectedly onto the train, waved goodbye to my house through the window. As home shrank into the distance, its black roof became small and insignificant, and then, like the Empties themselves, invisible.

***

We reached the payment station. This time, instead of being instructed to sit and wait in turn in a loop of seats pressed against the internal perimeter of the old church hall, the shadows were leading people off into side rooms with gusto. Scratchy, irksome black patches flitted back and forth, tired humans with their fingers rammed in their ears in a useless quest for silence following like sad sheep. The mass of black static chaperoning me pooled on the floor by my feet and screeched, '*follow*'. So follow I did. Through a side door, down a corridor. Unseen claws shimmied me into a tiny, make-shift cubicle and instructed me to lie on the narrow bed.

"Left or right. One, two, three, four, five. Four or five. One, two, three, four, or five?" Christ alive, why did it have to manifest such hideous sounds and speak in echoes?

"I'm sorry, I'm not sure what you mean," I replied, my index fingers thrust as plugs in my ears.

"Left or right finger. Or toe. Finger. Or toe."

Sweet Jesus. I looked down at my hands and realised what it meant.

It wanted more than my blood—it wanted a digit too.

It wanted my fresh flesh and bone.

I stood up and moved to the door. I needed out. This was one step too far. The seemingly vacant unit shifted through me, glided from behind me to the door in front. This penetration of my core felt like a wave of acidic hellfire riding through every cell of my body. I gagged as its antimatter gushed through my muscles and bones. It made it to the door before I could and I watched in despair as the bolt slammed across.

"Fingers or Toes. Left or Right. Right," it said again. A leather fedora hat which had been sat atop a small corner table flew up into the air, came to rest mid-air, shoulder height. I watched, frozen to the spot, as the hat floated back across the room. "You must choose. Internet fee gone up. No tissue payment, no internet, no life."

I sat back down on the gurney bed, my heart bashed like a jailed bird. No life? Did it mean this in the literal sense? Was I to die today if I didn't succumb to its demands? Or was it somehow aware of how much I valued my gaming time, how trivial my existence would become without my virtual stage? Either way, the door was locked, I was trapped. I could feel its revolting nothingness brushing up and down against my thigh, keen for my answer. I had no choice. It wasn't going to let me leave and I needed the internet—I spent over sixteen hours a day doing virtual gigs, touring the world with Cream, performing to massive crowds, all from the comfort of my living room. I had nothing else, no-one else. Without the internet, would I even exist? Betwixt a rock and a hard place was where I was wedged—I just hoped it, the Empty, wasn't going to *use* a rock and a hard place to take this heavy payment.

I shuffled my butt back onto the loose sheet of blue medical paper towel atop the wheeled bed, braced myself and, through gritted teeth, replied: "Left toe."

I clenched my fists and held my breath in preparation. Imprinted on my retina, before I screwed my eyes closed, was the snapshot of a floating, dipped fedora hat and a levitating hacksaw.

***

I screamed for ages, bled for ages. The Empty tossed a bunch of bandages at me, unbolted the door and left. I stemmed the flow of blood from my foot with shaking hands, watching a floating hat escort away with my toe on a small dish.

I wrapped my foot. The bandage became red soaked in an instant. I grabbed another roll from the medical trolley and wrapped and re-wrapped the wound until the bleeding eased. I hopped back to the station that day, through sideways sleet, onto the train, a mess of blood and rain and tears and made my way back home.

***

I immersed myself in my VR performances for the rest of the week, my pain alleviated slightly by being on stage. I wondered how long a toe would buy me. Weeks? Maybe a month?

Ten days after the Empties first mutilated me, another knock came at my door.

That Empty was wearing a necktie with the symbol of an upturned cross on it. I followed its scuffle of a shadow, its hovering black noose, down the road, onwards towards the train station. I psyched myself up to say goodbye to the little toe on my right foot this time. My left foot stump had started to dry and scab over. Four toes per foot wasn't the end of the world. I could deal with that. In a couple of hours, I'd be back at home, in my living room, on stage at Glastonbury Festival thrashing out 'Deserted Cities of the Heart' and 'Sunshine of My Love' to thousands of virtual, smiling fans.

That time they kept me in overnight. I was paralysed by the medication they'd forced upon me, yet able to witness and feel every scrape and cut the floating scalpel made, I had no option but to watch them hack off my entire foot and imbibe bag after bag of my lifeblood. Each time one of them downed a gulp, I'd see an evil body cloud up, become

38

vermillion fog before my eyes. Some of them started to look a little less empty. Instead of shadows cast beneath spaces of nothingness, through drugged eyes, I swear I sore fleshy, flitting, geometric shapes. Organic. Fluid. Peach, pink, brown and cream. Edges, angles, corners and planes. Dustings of rose. Blockish, translucent organic apparitions sloped from room to room as I bawled in agony. Was the pain making me delusional? Many of the shapes were wearing black baseball caps, black beanie hats, studded leather jackets. One had draped over its shifting image a Darkthrone t-shirt held together with safety pins.

My entire leg throbbed. Pain pin-balled up my left hand side from where my foot was once attached. Shock punched me in the gut. I yelled a hopeless, *'help me'* from the hospital bed but I received no help, just a hard, thick slap around the jaws from a flush-tint, cuboid, Empty appendage.

"Shut up. Shut up. Shut up," it screeched, echoed by ten-fold more of its allies. Fear stapled my mouth closed. "Be quiet or no anaesthetic next time. Next time."

Next time? I yanked out the pouch and needle which had been drilled into a vessel near my groin. It seemed to be replacing my body fluids with something dark, something made of nightmares, something I knew I didn't want or need inside of me. I lobbed it on the floor and then vomited hard into a cardboard kidney dish.

***

And there was a next time. Against my will and from a pit of unimaginable pain, I bid goodbye to my other foot. That debilitating loss bought me a knock-free month. But then they came again. They broke into my home, pulled me out from under my bed where I'd hidden—I was petrified, still feverish, battling an infection from the last amputation. They dragged me to the payment centre, knocked me out for twelve hours. My last memory before that surgery was of a floating chiffon Victoriana evening gown, matched velour gloves and a disposable medical mask screeching orders at me in tones of death whilst tethering me down to the wheeled bed. That time, they told me they'd removed a kidney, half of my lung, my right eye and a large section of my liver.

When I came round, I was on the train. I was propped up in a wheel chair when I regained consciousness, sat under the semi-clothed, black-grey cloud of an Empty; the Darkthrone fan. The train rolled to a stop and it pushed me along, all the while whistling a shrill, gut-splitting note from its invisible lips. Each toot it made felt like a woodpecker hammering on my eardrums. Disharmonious vibrations emanating from it shook and irritated each throbbing part of my sore, pained body. I was a shell of a man. It wheeled me back home and tipped me out onto my sofa with a bag of medication and comestibles.

"Aftercare package, package," it hollered and left.

I felt like I was dying. I did nothing but sleep and clamber to the kitchen for water for what felt like eternity, all the while spinning in and out of consciousness until I managed to muster up the energy to haul my frail body over to the VR screen. I pressed my nose up against the cold black mirror and switched it on. Thank God for VR, an escape from my world of pain. Within a second, I was back on stage, my boys behind me, able one more time to belt out the classic rock hits. Performance euphoria washed over me. The myriad of injuries and incisions the 'surgeons' had left all over my body for a moment, fell numb.

**

Three long months passed before they called again. An Empty knocked, screeched at me in power chords and wheeled me to the train station. Another Empty with a hint of peach to its nebulous form knocked me out with its Luciferous knuckles and a syringe of black static. When I came round, one of the b'stards told me they'd taken everything that was left to take from within the cavity of my abdomen. I screamed and screamed. It thrust a horrific, leather-gloved limb out at me which struck me solid. I recoiled in further pain, silenced.

They didn't understand—organs did not replenish as blood did. Yes, the liver had the weak ability to re-generate partially, but not as fast as they had been reaping slices of it from me. I felt like death warmed up. My hair had all fallen out. I had just one eye; I could feel no teeth were left. My arms were like drumsticks, bare bones. My hands and feet were long gone. I felt like a tipped-up sack.

In my delirious state of agony as an Empty wheeled and tipped me out back into my front room, I noticed something. The Empty—it appeared to have a human shape. A humanoid outline, human legs dressed in human trousers, peachy arms and hands, a torso wearing something woven, soft, possibly angora, in a shade of bruised blue. Under the cap which perched on what I imagined must've been its head, was a writhing bonce of tangled long, midnight black hair which whipped about like Medusa's snakes and a pair of soulless eyes filled with loathing.

"Cheerio," it said, its voice no longer resonant, no longer overly loud, no reverb—just human. I didn't have the strength to reply, every breath hurt. I swear as it left, it winked at me and smirked.

I collapsed on the sofa, slept. When I awoke, I scrabbled about, half on, half off the sofa, to retrieve the bag of pain relief, rationed food and water it'd hurled into my home as it left. Days passed, I felt weak, feverish, certain that death was near. Had I given up? I felt sure my end was nigh. Despite this overwhelming feeling of impending doom, I wanted, needed, to spend my last few days, hours, doing the one thing I loved before dropping off for the Big Sleep. So, doped up on pain relief, I hauled myself to my screen. Could I muster the energy to check in on my band? See the boys; hear the crowds cheer with joy just one more time? I pressed my nose up against the black screen and stretched for the 'on' button.

Nothing. Nothing happened. After flicking the button back and forth several times, I realised something was wrong.

It can't have run out already, the internet. I'd only just made a payment and that payment had been a rather substantial one, judging by how terrible I felt. I'd a vague memory of bartering with the Empty surgeon. I'd allowed it to take the last metre of my intestine, the final lobe of my liver, the other one of my kidneys in exchange for infinite internet. That's when I realised. That's when it clicked. I hadn't thought it through. Silly, foolish me. *What an idiot,* I thought, sat there in my white room, drowning in tears of pain and pure frustration—I hadn't made a payment for electricity.

It'd been cut off. And the internet wouldn't work without electricity. I couldn't delve into my VR world. I couldn't stand on stage, complete, with all my virtual organs, limbs, appendages, and drill out Cream classics to baying crowds of fans. Ginger Rogers would bang on his drum skins unaccompanied by the thrashing of the battle axe. Jack Bruce's lyrics would sound hollow without my guitar melodies accompanying him. I pressed my nose again and again against the black mirror of my VR entertainment system, hopeful I was mistaken. Again and again, harder and harder. Frustrated, furious, throbbing with pain, fear, anger. I opened what I felt was my one remaining eye and looked into the black mirror of the dead VR set in front of me—

—to be met with no reflection.

No face.

No sallow, concave cheeks, no glazed, tired eye, no strands of haywire, desperate hair stuck out from my scalp. No scalp. No neck, no shoulders. Biting down on the inside of my cheek to hold in screams of anguish, I drew myself up onto my bleeding, oozing sore stumps—and could not see any of them. I could see any of me in the dark reflective screen, none of me at all. I was nothing. I had become nothing. I was gone, empty.

I threw the space where my body should be back onto my sofa and screamed an acidic scream which echoed and bounced around the four ever-pressing walls. I sat my nothingness down in a pile of misery, invisible and alone.

My living room walls were painted white. My ceiling, which stretched out above me, was as white as a bed sheet and the floor below was all whitewashed boards. It was the whitest room in my house yet, in the final moment, before I lost my mind completely, it felt exponentially dark. It was as if a three-foot-deep, thick padding of virgin snow surrounded me, made a death's row prisoner of me. I wish I'd never opened my front door.

Almost incandescent and with the weight of infinity, my own four white walls pushed in.

And trapped within them, I have become nothing but a thunderous shadow, an eternal, black metal scream.

Bloodlust

E. S. Sibbald

Weaponry filled the shed from wall to wall. Blades and guns were lined neatly across tabletops, crossbows hung from the walls, grenades overflowed from carefully stacked crates. Bulk bought bags of salt leant against each other in a meticulously engineered pyramid. Prayer beads, crucifixes and jars of neatly labelled roots and powders filled long wooden shelves fixed to the wall.

The shed, despite its name, was more akin to a hollowed-out cabin. The walls were dark stained oak, the floor rough timber. Yellowing pamphlets and newspapers covered every window.

It had been the fixation of Kasper's dreams for months and finally seeing it left him slack-jawed with awe.

A large hand gripped Kas's shoulder. "Impressive, isn't it?"

"Sure is."

Uncle Walter's eyes flashed with pride. "Your old man would be over the moon to see you here. You know that?"

"I know," Kas said. It had been the first thing his mother said to him when he sat down at breakfast. Not *good morning*, not *happy birthday*, but *you'll make your father proud today*.

For centuries, the Bayats had kept a tradition; on the night of his sixteenth birthday, each boy born to the family killed his first monster. Tonight was Kasper's turn.

Uncle Abraham stood with his eldest son, Luca, discussing the specifications of a gun as they passed it between themselves.

His second son, Elias, sharpened a blade against a whetstone, the loud scrape of the metal echoing in the cavernous space.

Adam, Uncle Walter's only child, who had turned sixteen only four months earlier, sat on an overturned crate, scratching sullenly at a scab on his wrist.

"What are we expecting tonight?" asked Elias.

"Not certain. There's been reports of drained animals, so likely vampires, or chupacabras. A lost impundulu."

Elias grinned. "You've got an exciting night ahead of you, Kas. Bloodsuckers always make for a good chase."

"Kas. Here." An intricate belt lay reverently across Luca's open palms. "Uncle Karl gave it to me when I turned sixteen, but it doesn't fit me anymore. I want you to have it. Think of it as the gift he's not here to give you."

Kasper took the belt and ran his palms across the harsh brown leather, then trailing his fingertips over the frayed stitching. "Thank you."

Luca nodded and showed Kasper how to put it on. One band buckled around his waist like a regular belt and a second piece ran diagonally across his torso like a seatbelt. Luca pointed at each strap and pouch and explained what they were designed to hold – stakes, bullets, daggers, a gun – filling each compartment as he did until Kas had a small arsenal strapped to his body.

"Here." Elias hung a string of solid silver prayer beads around Kas's neck. "Tuck it into your shirt."

Kas did as he was told, cringing at the bite of ice-cold metal against his skin.

A tin canopy beside the shed sheltered a battered seven-seat Range Rover. It might have once been green, but layers of mud and grimy stains made it impossible to be sure.

Kas's uncles sat in front, Elias and Luca in the middle row and he in the back with Adam.

Adam seemed different, smaller somehow since joining the hunt. Deep purple crescents ringed his eyes and he moved slower, as if in a daze. A sour grimace replaced the confident toothy grin that had once camped on his face.

Kas didn't mention it.

"Excited?" Elias grinned over the headrest.

"Sure."

"I remember my first hunt," he said. "Werewolves. There was a pack of six and we got 'em all. Your dad killed two and the rest of us got one each. I still keep mine with me." He brushed his fingers over the hood of his jacket. It was fur-lined – grey, streaked with dark tuffs of brown. "For luck."

Kasper's stomach lurched. Elias always wore that jacket. "But aren't werewolves... people?"

"Not at all," cut in Uncle Abraham. "They traded their humanity for monstrosity."

"Don't they turn back?"

"On the outside, maybe, but not inside."

Kasper had seen a werewolf transform once, in a video Elias had filmed on a hunt. The creature looked exactly like a person until its teeth narrowed into sharp points and the hair on its arms grew thick and coarse, burying every inch of skin with fur.

He looked back at Elias's jacket and shuddered. He imagined the soft fur lining of the coat replaced with human skin. Kasper squeezed his eyes shut against the intrusive image, focusing on the dark insides of his eyelids for the remainder of the journey.

The car finally rolled to a stop at the edge of a tangled bushland reserve, kept closed for conservation.

The uncles explained that while what they were hunting likely didn't live amongst the trees full-time, the reserve bordered most of the homes where pets had been reported dead or missing and one large farm that had lost large numbers of cattle and sheep, so it likely served as part of a hunting ground.

Uncle Abraham opened the trunk of the car, removed a long rifle and passed it to Luca. He then lifted out a rusty metal cage the size of a milk crate. Inside the cage, a large rabbit with white and black mottled fur sat comfortably, despite the small space. It stared through the bars with calm eyes, nose twitching in a lazy rhythm.

"What's that for?" Kasper asked.

"Bait. To lure out the monsters." Abraham placed the cage on the floor and removed the rabbit, cradling it against his chest.

Elias nudged Kasper with his elbow. "Get out your knife."

"What?"

"Didn't Luca pack you any blades?"

Kas pulled back the canvas jacket he wore over his t-shirt and the belt. Two medium-sized daggers sat snug against his hip, one regular carbon steel and the other silver. They were identical in width and length but easily differentiable by their handles, one sleek and plain, the other intricately carved with words in a language he didn't know.

"Take it out."

Kas brushed his shaking fingers over the handles.

"Just steel's fine."

Kasper freed the dagger, his movements slow and careful. His family's eyes were locked on him, unblinking, except for Adam, who gazed at the ground where he had dug a ditch in the soil with the toe of his boot.

Abraham stepped closer to Kas, his fingers absently brushing the rabbit's hair. "Not too deep," he said, "just enough to put the scent of blood in the air."

Kasper's face stared back at him, reflected in the smooth black eye of the rabbit. He could see the glint of the knife, a streak of glowing white against the darkness.

"Go on," pressed Luca.

Kas held the knife flat against the rabbit's flank. It remained still, oblivious to what was happening and Kas felt his stomach twist.

"We don't have all night," Elias said, a sharp edge in his voice making the words sound like a warning.

The rabbit's flesh quivered under the blade as Kas slowly applied more pressure, until all at once the skin split and red spilt from the creature's side in long beading rivulets.

The rabbit screamed – a dreadful sound, something between the sharp shrill of a bird and the cry of a human child. The creature's body heaved with breath and its eyes grew large as it struggled against Abraham's coat.

"Ready?"

The pounding of Kas's heart in his ears drowned out the responses of his family.

Abraham threw the rabbit to the ground. It scrambled in the dirt, stirring up a small cloud of dust before bolting into the blackness of the trees.

A firm hand wrapped around Kasper's arm and the world tilted violently as he was pulled forward, the bush morphing into a blurry rush of shadows. His boot collided with a bump in the ground and he stumbled.

"Careful!" scolded Luca beside him. "Eyes up."

Kas's head snapped up. In the distance, he could see a blur of white against the night as if a beam of moonlight had slipped through the canopy of trees above and taken a physical form. The rabbit.

The family halted to watch the creature from a short distance.

It was still, half-hidden behind a low shrub, eyes blown wide, watching for danger as it licked its blood-matted fur. Kas was almost certain rabbits could see in the dark and he wondered what it saw when it looked at him, the boy who had hurt it. Surely he was nothing less than a monster in its mind.

A branch snapped and Luca's hand tightened on Kas's arm. He was sure that tomorrow there would be a ring of bruises printed on his skin.

Two white eyes appeared in the dark over the rabbit. They were familiar from every nature documentary Kas had ever seen – the eyes of a predator.

The longer he stared, the more the creature began to take shape, shifting into place like smoke, the shape of it like a void against an already black backdrop. It bent closer to the rabbit, inspecting it until, in one quick flurry of movement, the rabbit was off the ground and clutched tightly in shadowy hands.

A burst of brightness flooded the bush. Uncle Walter had ignited a flare. A great volcano of flame erupted from its top, painting the world red, leaking out smoke that circled the hunter's feet.

In the light, Kas could now clearly see what had picked up the rabbit. It looked *almost* human. Its eyes, no longer bursts of white, were a dull brown, tinted red by the glow of the flare. It wore a grey tank top and a dirty pair of denim jeans. If not for the lifeless rabbit clutched in its hands, the messy streaks of blood tracing its chin and the fangs Kas knew were obscured behind its red lips, it could have been mistaken for a young woman.

The creature paused, taking in the men surrounding it, the hungry glint in their eyes, the guns and stakes and crossbows strapped across their bodies. It didn't take long to realise the situation it had found itself in. The rabbit dropped to the floor like a wet rag and the creature bolted.

The hunt was back on.

"Get your knife out, Kas!" Luca panted between breaths as they ran.

"Silver one this time!" added Elias.

Kas fumbled at the knives in his belt, releasing the heavier one with the intricate handle from its sheath. He held it tight, determined not to let it slip from his sweaty grasp.

Kas had never been athletic and his lungs felt hollowed out from running. Every exhale released air, but with every inhale he tasted blood. The fear of what might be said to him if he gave up here on his first hunt propelled him forward.

"Adam!" called Uncle Walter. "Shoot it, but don't kill it!"

Adam pulled a crossbow from a holster on his back and loaded an arrow into it. He held it steady against the jostle of his body, lifted the bow with ease and released the bolt.

The arrow landed in the thick trunk of a tree with a crack.

Luca snatched the crossbow from Adam's hands and elbowed him hard enough he fell to the ground.

It took only a moment for Luca to release a second arrow. It flew through the air and plunged into the bloodsucker's calf.

The creature fell to the ground and Kas couldn't help but wince. He knew it was a monster, but it fell just like any person would. Its body crumpled in on itself, arms covering its face for protection, a frightened and pained yelp leaving its lips.

Kas tore his eyes from the bloody heap on the floor, searching instead for Adam. He was curled into his thick parka, holding one of his knees at an odd angle.

Kas only made it one step towards his cousin before two hands slowly come to curl around Adam's upper arms. They yanked hard and with a shriek, Adam was pulled, withering, into the trees.

Two more monsters melted out of the shadows and hauled away the creature Luca had shot.

There was more than one monster in this bush with them and the possibility that they might be outnumbered gnawed at Kas. He had only a moment to process this information before the Bayat family were sprinting again.

"They took Adam!" Kas shouted.

"We'll get him back!"

Uncle Walter's flare had dwindled to a dull glow, hardly illuminating even silhouettes anymore. Kas didn't dare blink, afraid he may lose sight of Elias, who was almost lost in the darkness only a metre ahead. Tree branches scratched at his face and a rock had found its way into his shoe where it stabbed his heel with every pounding step. Kas clutched the handle of the silver blade with his sweaty palm like it was the only thing keeping his consciousness tethered to his aching body.

"Hold!"

Kas froze, almost tripping over the undergrowth with the suddenness of it. His heart beat hard against his ribcage and he swung his head wildly, seeking out his uncle's voice.

A second flare lit up the night. The red glow illuminated a group of monsters standing directly ahead of the hunters. There were four in total – still one less than the remaining members of the Bayat family. But they had fangs, and flashing eyes and could move faster than anything Kas had ever seen and between them, they had a tight grip on a very frightened Adam.

Adam fought against the hands holding him, thrashing his arms, kicking his uninjured leg so violently in the dirt that he dug a canal into the ground.

Uncle Walter moved first, stepping forward and raising his crossbow in one fluid movement. The bow was loaded with a sharpened stake – he had modified it himself. "Step away from my son."

"Drop your weapons," said the monster, which looked like a young woman. Blood still dripped from where Luca had shot it, though the wound was already shallower than it had been.

Counter to its words, more weapons were raised in defiance; a crossbow loaded with silver-tipped arrows in Luca's large hands, a homemade flamethrower in Elias's and a pair of twin stakes in Abraham's. Kas held his knife.

The creature's mouth split into a grin, showing off two sharp canines. In one quick movement, it twisted its fingers in Adam's hair and with a hard yank, pulled his head back and buried its face in his neck. It drank deeply for only a few seconds before pulling back and lifting its wrist to its mouth, which it cut open with one of its fangs before thrusting the bloody stream against Adam's lips.

Elias ignited his flame thrower, a burst of fire blasting from the nozzle, hot enough that Kas could feel its warmth through his jacket. One of the monsters caught alight, screaming and stumbling into one of its brethren, lighting up the second creature like kindling as they both crashed to the floor. The air filled with the stench of over charred meat.

The remaining two vampires quickly forgot Adam, letting his body collapse on the ground in favour of lunging at the hunters.

Kas froze when his eyes met with one of the monsters. It grinned, and Kas knew he looked like easy prey. While his family fought, brutal with their weapons, he shivered with fear, the small dagger clutched desperately in front of him with both hands.

The creature charged at him, arms swinging wildly, its fingers curled into claws. The dagger was useless. By the time the monster was close enough for him to use the short blade, it would have already gouged out Kas's eyes or torn open his throat, so instead of fighting, Kas ducked, letting his body go slack and plummeting down as quick as he could. Something hard hit him in the head – the creature's elbow. It hurt, but no worse than if he had walked into a door frame. A level of pain he could easily tolerate.

Further from the monster now, Kasper sprung back to his feet, stumbling backwards into something solid. He turned, finding himself face to face with Uncle Abraham.

"Don't run from it, Kas!" Abraham shouted, his eyes wild as he pushed Kas away from him, back towards the monster. "Kill the bastard!"

Kasper turned his attention back to the monster, just in time to see a silver arrow fly through the back of its head and out its eyeball, the socket sizzling where the pure metal had touched, a burst of black sludge spilling from the hole. Silver wasn't enough to kill a vampire. but it certainly hurt.

The creature turned its attention away from Kas, directing its attack instead towards Uncle Walter, who had shot at it.

Kas stumbled back, grateful for his uncle's kindness – if that is what it had been. More likely it was simply an act of faithlessness in him to man up and kill something as was expected of him.

Kas crouched on the ground, bringing his arms over his head, one fist still holding the knife and the other fisted into his hair, tugging hard on the strands to ground himself. Everything feels like too much; each burst of light from Elias's flamethrower like a flash grenade behind his eyelids, every scream a siren.

Through the gap between his elbows, Kasper watched Uncle Walter fire another arrow through the monster's head. Before it could recover, he loaded another arrow with unbelievable speed and fired it into the creature's neck. Then another through its shoulder, and a fifth through the fleshy part of its cheek as it turns away heading for the trees, having realised this is a fight it couldn't win. Dark coagulated blood dripped thick and gooey from each of its wounds.

Kas's stomach lurched and he removed one hand from where it was tangled in his hair to cover his mouth, but it did nothing to stop the vomit rising up his throat, coating his hand in chunks of half-digested food and stomach acid. The stench of it burned his nostrils and his eyes stung with tears.

The final creature had vanished, disappeared back into the trees. Kas watched the other Bayat men as they walked deeper into the thicket, taunting the beast, calling it a coward, telling it to come back and fight. He hoped desperately it wouldn't.

"I'll be home soon," Kas whispered, repeating the words to himself like a mantra.

"Kasper! Look out!"

Two hands dug into his shoulders from behind and pulled him down before pinning him to the ground.

The creature snarled at him, fangs sharp and white in the moonshine. It held one hand to Kas's throat and with the other, yanked off the prayer beads around his neck, throwing them far across the dirt with a sharp yelp of pain at the contact with a blessed artifact.

The monster bent its head and Kas felt something sharp like a needle going into his neck. Struggling was useless, the creature was too strong.

It was going to drain him dry, just as it had done to all those cattle and sheep from the farms.

Kas heard the sound of a blade freeing from its sheath and, in one smooth movement, Luca sliced off the monster's head. It fell to the ground with a thump, rolling a short way through the dirt, leaving a snail trail of viscera. The headless corpse of the creature fell forward, winding Kas completely with the force and splattering his face with rancid blood and filling his mouth with the taste of bitter salt and iron.

Kas desperately scrambled backwards, shoving the heavy body away. Black goo continued to seep from its neck, pooling thickly on the floor like mud.

Shame shrouded Kasper like a thick coat. He had failed his first hunt spectacularly. The first Bayat for generations to break the tradition. If his father were alive to see him today, he would be so disappointed.

When he lifted his gaze, Kas expected to see that same shame in his family's eyes, but no one was looking at him. All eyes were on Adam writhing on the ground, his spine pressed up against a tree while he clawed at his shirt, scuffing and tearing the fabric with his fingernails. His veins were a shocking shade of purple under his sweat-soaked papery skin. His body heaved as if retching and he screamed in halting gasps.

"They got him," Elias said, his voice grave and hollow.

Adam threw his head back in a violent fit of coughs that turned to choking. Two small white shapes tumbled out of his mouth and onto the

58

ground. Teeth. A steady stream of blood flooded his mouth and beneath the red, two sharp white points protruded slightly from his gums – his fangs already growing in.

"Kasper," said Uncle Abraham, matching the same tone of voice Elias had spoken in. "Do you have your weapons?"

He nodded. The knife had slipped his grip in the struggle with the final beast but everything else was still strapped to the belt.

"Then stand up."

He did.

"You still haven't made your first kill." Abraham eyed him meaningfully.

Uncle Walter made a noise like a wounded animal and his knees buckled beneath him though he didn't fall to the ground.

The other men were all silent. The trees were still, no sign of the earlier wind rustling through. Even nature had frozen, waiting, watching.

"Finish the job." Uncle Abraham nodded his head towards Adam, whose eyelids were fluttering violently, his body convulsing as if he were having a seizure.

"What?"

"Use a stake. Through his – *its* heart."

Kas looked to his other uncle, Adam's father. He was now holding Elias's hand so tight that tendons and veins visibly bulged along his arm. Tears streamed down his face from wide eyes, but he didn't object.

"But it's Adam."

Abraham shook his head. "No, it isn't, lad. Not anymore."

Kas looked to each member of his family, hoping one of them would stop this, tell him it was okay, promise he didn't have to do this, that none of them would *ever* do this, they were a family. The first rule of the hunt was that they stuck together, no Bayat was left behind to fight alone. Walter and Elias avoided his eyes, Luca only nodded once.

Each step felt like walking through a dream, thick and syrupy. Bile rose in his throat and Kas forced it down as he knelt beside his cousin.

Adam was still now. It looked like he was already dead; his chest no longer moving with breath. The wave of grief Kas felt was threaded with a guilty undercurrent of relief. He won't have to kill him after all.

The tension began to drain from Kas's muscles and he took a steadying breath.

Adam's eyes flash open. His deep brown irises were ringed by a circle of blood red. He lunged forward and Kas wedged the stake in his chest, pushing it deeper until it was buried almost entirely in Adam's body.

The creature that had once been his cousin retched and heaved violently one final time before falling back to the ground, finally, completely dead.

Abraham walked behind Kas and pulled the stake from the corpse before helping him to his feet. "You did good." He plunged two fingers into the hole in Adam's chest and they came away sticky with blood, still red, not having yet turned rotten and old like the blood that had poured from the other monsters. He smeared it in a line down Kas's forehead, starting at his hairline under his fringe, and ending between his eyebrows. Then on each side of his face, lining the shallow ridges of his cheekbones.

The smell of the blood was strong. Distracting. It flooded all of Kas's senses and he wanted nothing more than to wipe it from his face, get the taste out of his lungs, clear away the reminder of what he has done.

"Let's get you back home." Abraham clapped him on the shoulder and lead him back through the forest. The family walked in silence, their heavy steps singing Adam's funeral march.

A chill settled over Kas's skin and he thought the adrenaline from the hunt must be wearing off. He popped the collar on his jacket and pulled it tight against his body.

They piled into the car, Elias taking the back seat with Kas, where Adam had sat on the drive in. "Are you alright?" he asked. "You look really pale."

Kas shrugged. "Just tired. Upset." He felt ill. Wrong. "It was a big night."

Elias nodded and turned towards the window, giving as much space as he could in the back seat of a car.

Kas tugged his jacket tighter like a blanket. Even with the heating on, he could feel ice running through his veins. Slowly, to not draw attention to the movement, he snaked a hand up to his neck and pressed his fingers against the skin there. He could feel twin wounds like pin-pricks from when the monster had leapt on top of him, already scabbing over.

He clenched his fists in his lap and tried to ignore the coppery taste coating his tongue as the tingling of a deep, relentless craving settled in.

Slow March Meal Plan

Rickey Rivers Jr.

My first one was more difficult than the second. The third was docile until the end. All of them served a purpose, as all people must. I'm sure you've heard of temporary insanity. It's also been deemed the insanity defense. People like to give names to things, to classify them, to place them in neat little boxes. But you can't put every manner of person in a box. We simply don't fit.

I remember reading a story about a group of passengers who were stranded out to sea. They seriously considered eating one another after the food had run out. They were rescued before the group resulted to killing and eating one of their own. Now, suppose they weren't? How long would it take you to consider actually eating another person?

On my first time I proposed temporary cannibalism, an idea that makes sense given the circumstances. But I have no grand tale to tell. I simply partook due to interest. You see, I've always been curious. People and curiosity go hand in hand. Unlike cats, curiosity doesn't necessarily kill. I suppose it can, but anything can kill the unwilling mind. And a mind must be willing to go far enough, to be able to hunt, as our ancestors did, to catch a smaller creature. And what creature is smallest in the human eye, bipedal, developing as we do? You know which I mean.

My first hunt was ten years ago. I like to space them out. Rushing leads to mistakes. No matter how delicious eventuality is you must not result to rushing. You have to take your time. Time is all we have. It's the most fleeting. A little bit wasted is a lot in reflection. Time is precious, most certainly. I've wasted time eating junk for years.

Food of today is full of preservatives, salt and added sugars. Older people say it wasn't always like that, but I think it was. They've pumped chickens with more and more hormones. Genetic mutation is the goal. Scientists work hard pretending they aren't purposely trying to change human DNA. But we've all been changing slowly. Bit by bit, every day we eat bull from the stores. Everything's genetically enhanced. No wonder we're getting sicker and sicker. It only makes sense to grow your own food. That way you insure you're ingesting the pureness of the Earth, through fruits and veggies.

And the Earth is only so pure now, because people keep polluting it. There's trash everywhere and people don't care. Why hurt the planet you live on? It makes no sense. Now these rich folks wanna leave Earth and go elsewhere. Who cares about the problems here right? Who cares about the little guy, his little wife and family?

Never had much of a family, never cared for one either. Family or friend, friend or foe, they're all people and people let you down. I'm not a nihilist either, just a realistic. I've lived many a year. I've seen people change. Folks act funny for a little bit of money. Every day the greed grows. You'd think it rained money. Money doesn't grow on trees, but people will quickly put you in the dirt for a little bit of what you have, like you can merge with the soil and help the next generation.

We're not trees. We're people. We don't help the next generation. We're selfish. That's all people have ever been. Just selfish folks trying to tell young folks what to think and feel and believe, selfish folks wanting to stay in office, getting old, never want to leave, false promises of progress, it's all a joke, a big joke and we're at the center: people, people eating people. That's all we do.

Some cultures actually do this beyond the metaphor. They consume the flesh of others. I've heard tell of people in the upper echelon partaking in the practice. Is it a sick idea or worthwhile one? If your belief is immortality or a quicker way to power, then I'm sure the idea intrigues you. Me, I don't care about living forever or gaining power. I'm not trying to gain any kind of position in this sick society. I eat what I eat, and I like it.

Preserving pieces is the possible obstacle. I've had to throw parts out before. It's a terrible thing, because so many people are starving today. And our government for sure doesn't care to help them or feed them. Everything's all about work. You're not worth anything to anyone else if you're not working or tired from work or going to school to graduate and work a job you don't care about while paying off student loans. People want you paying permanently. There's no time for rest.

There's barely time to make your bed much less sleep in it. The bed is your foundation. You work your whole life for a nice bed and you can barely sleep in it. You have to work for the sheets, a good pillow and to even pay off the bed. Don't you dare forget heating and air, much less the bed you ultimately die in. It's all about spending; keep spending in this money-led society.

Everybody works. Nobody eats. We just think we eat, but we're not comfortable. We're only pushing food in. Guzzling the greed the last generation left us with, because some of those folks refuse to leave positions of power. They perpetually wish to remain in charge. If immortality existed they'd be the first ones to sign up.

They'd love to remain in power for centuries. They crave power. They simply require it to survive. They love telling others what to do. They love being in charge. They don't wish to bridge gaps. They want age gaps to widen. They think age and wisdom go hand in hand. It doesn't. Old doesn't equal wise. Old is old. You can be old and dumb. I've met plenty of old and dumb people. It's okay to be dumb, but simply admit it. Admit you're dumb. Admit you don't know what you're talking about all the time. You're not wise. People just show you respect by quieting their own voice when you speak. That doesn't mean you're actually saying anything interesting. You an old person speaking at the end of the day, step down. Be quiet. Quit hogging the spotlight and be a grand person already.

***

I've strayed so far from my original point. The delicacy of eating outside the lines, as your mind is also outside the proverbial box of mediocracy. Away with the store bought food, embrace the home grown. This is not to say I don't use any store bought anything, I do. I shop. I'm a regular person. It's just the added salts, sugars, hormones, you know. I try to stay healthy. I like eating children.

I've kept recipes in my head. They've kept me on track. Momma always said I could be a chef. I used to cook for her. It's fun to cook for people you care about, seeing their faces light up when they see and smell the food. Speaking of smell, there's no hassle with the right seasonings. I've had toes before, chopped and seasoned with basil, paprika, garlic, onion and a dash of brown sugar. I know, sugar is bad, forgive me.

It's really quite a snack once it's finished. You fry them up in a pan. They make a nice finger food, like those tiny sausages packaged together. Difference is you eat the meat around the bones.

***

It's interesting to be in between age groups. I've always felt a kind of alienation. Expressing myself can often come with difficulties. I wasn't really a smart child, but I wasn't dumb either. I was average. It's okay to be average. People are obsessed with wanting to be more than, to be spectacular, to be amazing. In that sense I feel Shakespearian. To be or not to be doesn't matter. The only thing that matters is a sense of self. I have it. Do you?

***

I'm not dumb. I know my way is unusual. People don't like to talk about their private pleasures. But I do wish it weren't taboo to simply express your desires. My desires to eat have nothing to do with sexual pleasure or prowess. My desire to eat is natural, a human reaction; a curious mind realizing it can eat anything it pleases. And what pleases me, at least sensibility wise, is the consumption of children.

Now, why children? They simply taste better. I think it's the pureness of them. They haven't yet been tainted by this terrible world. I like under age ten. They're just the right age, the right flavor. Old people are much too ripe and middle-aged folks are full of regrets from their teenage years. Yes, you can taste that. In the same sense that a big game hunter can taste a deer's fear, you can taste a creature's sensibilities.

You can even taste hopes and dreams. I've had brain served with onions, garlic, bell peppers and seasonings. You can have delightful dreams after consuming the perfect creature. And what creature could be more perfect than a child, especially one from a good household, no abuse, no trauma, just the delicate taste of innocence? A fresh chicken, an unsullied cow, these are the beautiful things in life and the world we live in just a farm after all. We should eat and we should eat well.

I have no beliefs of sacrifice or using the blood for anything else. I don't want the blood. It's disposed of. You don't want chicken blood either. The meat is the flavor, the most important thing. Only taboos divide us. I've had three different races. I've tasted no differences.

***

Back when I lived with Momma things were different, but similar. We had cat named Millie. She was a tabby with a nice orange color. I loved that cat, but Momma didn't. She was scared, scared or jealous. It's interesting when people become jealous over you. When did I ever deserve jealousy? I was a kid.

I didn't understand a lot about life then, but I grew older and became slightly less confused about my placement in this world. I think I came to know myself further after riding with Momma one day. On that day we came across a man in military gear walking down the street. It was Veteran's Day. This man was walking slowly and he was holding a rifle.

"It's all right, son."

Momma said that. But she was looking at him. I'm not sure who she was talking to. The guy kept walking. His eyes were glazed. He seemed to be in a trance with a far off look. He reminded me of my army men action figures. He didn't seem scary. He seemed like he was still on a mission.

***

One time Millie got in Momma's way and Mom stepped on her paw by mistake. Millie made a loud yelp and Momma was real shook up. I laughed about it in private. It was funny. The whole house was lit was noise; Millie yelping, Momma screaming, the TV blaring. I remember a movie was on, something about a war. Momma liked war movies. I think when she watched them she thought about Dad. I think that's why she got me the army men action figures, too. I never asked for them, but presents are presents, parents are parents. You have to be thankful.

I was always thankful. I was thankful when I found Millie. She was on the street just walking, so I asked Momma to pull over the car. Millie didn't run or seem scared. She let me pick her up, and put her in the backseat. When we got home I gave her fresh milk.

Apparently you aren't supposed to give cats milk, but to me it made sense, because of cartoons. Cartoons taught me a lot. I liked Tom and Jerry, but Tom and Jerry didn't show the whole truth.

***

I got upset with Momma on a day of many days. I went outside and screamed. I'm surprised the neighbors didn't call the police. Then again, I'm not. My neighbors never much liked the police. I don't blame them. Nobody likes harassment. People liked to be left alone. I liked and like my own devices. I liked and like my own distractions. When I got distracted back in the day I'd take Millie outside and

70

run around the backyard. It was fun, fresh air, no noise, no Momma.

Sometimes you need no Momma, just to feel alive. I didn't realize that when I was a boy. When I was a boy I was dumber. I'm different now. I'm better than a boy could be, but I could never regain my purity.

***

I lost my purity when Momma died. I'd like to say I ended her, but that wouldn't be right. I took my frustrations out on Millie. I threw her against a brick wall and stomped her out until she stopped moving. I didn't want to. I wanted an anger release. And it made sense to hurt a pet rather than hurt a person. I don't ever hurt people. Even the kids, I've never actually hurt them. I feed them before anything is cut. I make sure they sleep well. It's important to have a good sleep, especially when it's your final one. And kids everywhere deserve a good rest. The world is stressful and full of pain. I said that to Momma too.

***

I make sure to use every piece I tear away. I don't want children to suffer. That's why the good home plan works. They must come from good homes. They have to be pure. That's why it's been three children in ten years. It's harder and harder to find good children. I don't see how Santa does it. I guess that's why that myth was created. To ensure children are on their best behavior, but a lot of kids don't believe in him. And that's fine. I never did, either. But the good kids know there's a chance that Santa may be real, so they keep that dream alive in their heads.

In that sense, I'm thankful for myths. They comfort us when we're down. It's important to believe in something. When you believe you come to understand, to know. And I know that children are the ultimate gift. They can transfer happiness right into you. Energy transference: the innocent energy of children through marrow and meat. Never the blood, it's not right to drink blood from children. That would make you a demon.

***

I think about that army man sometimes. If I had left the car and walked up to him would he have shot me or spoke to me? Maybe he'd have some advice? I don't know. I wonder what he went through in life. What led him to walking down the street in fatigues with a rifle? As an adult the answer is obvious, the military itself. Something happened that changed his mind, warped it entirely. They say trauma changes the shape of the brain, trauma and depression. If that's the case everyone's walking around with weird shaped brains, everyone but the innocent ones, everyone who hasn't been exposed to the trauma of living.

And the trauma of living is a real thing. Believe you me. If you haven't gone through it you've only been lucky. Everyone goes through it eventually.

That's why it's important to get them young, eat them young. It's protection from a chaotic society, a sick world.

"It's the end times."

Momma said that time and time again. She said it when Daddy died and I think it's truer than ever years after. It's always been the end times. The end times keep going and going. They're like the good times that people want to keep going. But the good times are the times that actually end. The good times are fleeting. The bad days, the bad times, the final times are a constant. It's important to protect yourself at these times.

That's why the army man was walking his military walk down a lonely street. That's why Daddy died in a useless war. That's why Momma died choking. That's why Millie died squashed under a boot. It's the times we're living in. These times are the end. These children need not know the horrors of the world. The horrors of the world will scar them. They need to be taken out slowly, peacefully. No pain for the good ones.

Suffice to say it's been ten years since the first meal. And I know my purpose. I've staked out near a local school, not too close, but close enough. Some of the children don't walk in groups. It's important to find a child who doesn't take the bus. It's important to find a child who gets picked up.

Following is the only way, it's a process. It can take months to find the perfect meal. It's agonizing and exciting at the same time. It's watching the waiter bring food to every table but yours. It's getting up from your table and walking into the kitchen and taking your meal which you know you deserve. It's walking back to your table with the meal. It's salivating on the way home. It's ignoring the questions. It's feeding the meal. It's taking your time. It's all about time. But most of all, you must be discreet.

74

Hunters of the Desert Planet

Chris Marchant

I pull myself slowly from inside the wreckage. It's been days waiting for the scouting parties to return. Most of the crew left, in two different groups, one towards the distant hills, the other in the opposite direction. I was left, with another crew member, to watch over both the ship and the injured. We've tried to repair what we can, but the ship will never fly again. The emergency beacon is now transmitting, however it's doubtful that any ship will pick it up, unless that ship is in orbit. The signal is just too weak. Unless we can find a power source, we'll never get off this planet.

Movement catches my eye, it's not close, but it is approaching my position. I back into the shadows of our camp. The light from the two suns makes it difficult to hide. When we crashed, most of the ship was damaged in the collision. We were able to salvage a lot, which helped us extend a group of small caves nearby, making a secure camp. The remaining injured are inside, the ones we couldn't save are buried just outside, with the ones who died in the crash.

The runner is getting closer, I can now see some things chasing him. They look like giant slugs. He is struggling, the sand is fine and clings. He slides backwards and loses his footing. The sands cascades, spilling down and he goes with it.

Somehow it carries him past the hunters, who get caught up in the sand avalanche. They are swept away to the right, the runner is carried left. I stay hidden, watching, the injured have to be protected.

After a while, there's movement again, the slugs have recovered and are searching the area. It seems they can scent through the sand and they quickly narrow down an area and start digging. This is when I realise that the slugs had riders, when they dismount and help with the digging. It takes a short time for them to reach the runner and pull him out, he's fighting but the numbers are against him. They truss him up and attach him to the harness on one of the slugs, then they start moving away.

I stay there, watching and worrying about the search parties. This runner almost led the hunters to us, what if it happens again? We have no way to communicate with each other and we are low on supplies, especially water. I start slowly working my way back to the caves, the sand moving with every step. The slugs seemed to have the ability to track us, even in this desert environment. How could we avoid being tracked? I start thinking about ways to cover our scent, what would damage native earth slugs, would that work on alien slugs? What were the creatures riding the slugs? They weren't close enough for me to see.

Movement, in the distance. I squint, shading my eyes,. There again, rising and falling with the shift of the dunes. The glare on the sand makes it difficult to see anything that's not within shouting range. I scan the area, trying to identify what it was. Those hunters scared me and the unknown riders are even more frightening. Movement again, a head crests a dune. It's some kind of animal; it's long and has multiple limbs, which stabilise it on the sand. It's moving at an angle, it will pass me on the right, getting a bit closer before moving away once more. The gait is purposeful, is it heading for food, or water? The search parties went out for water, so if this animal can lead me to wate... I am torn, if I head back to let them know, I could lose it, if I don't and something happens they might never know. In the end, I do neither, I leave a message on the wall and set out to follow the animal.

The sand shifts easily, hiding tracks, so I would have lost the animal if I had delayed. Then the realisation dawns, I could lose myself and not be able to get back to the others. I have no compass, no way of communicating. I take deep breaths and fight down the panic. The caves are under the large hill, it's rock and can be seen for miles. It would be hard to lose that.

I was at risk of losing the creature, it has made a lot of progress and is nearly out of sight. I struggle, trying to catch up. The extra legs give it such an advantage, as it gets ever further away, but before I lose sight of it, there's a faint shadow ahead of it. It looks like rock, rising slightly above the endless sand. As I get closer, the size of it slowly increases and an area in front of it shimmers in the heat. Is it just caused by the heat, or could there be water there?

I start trying to move faster, but the arid heat is draining and I'm afraid of running out of water. The rock rises as I get closer, looming ominously from the sand. Dark in colour, with jagged peaks. Chills crawl down my spine; somehow I know that this is not a good place for my crew mates The hope of water is the only thing keeping my feet heading towards it.

The heat of the double suns bakes the sand, enough that it radiates back into the air, scorching my feet, My head pounds, even though a hat shades my face. Though one sun is close to setting, the rise of the third colours one side of the sky, the heat will be stifling until the first has set, hopefully I'll reach the shade before the third sun rises fully.

The shade is a shock after the heat of the suns. It feels like the warmth is being sucked out of my body and a bone deep chill is setting in. From here I can see movement and faint sounds reach my ears. Suddenly there's a series of growls coming from behind me, I crouch, ducking farther back into my patch of shade. Something runs past me, it's a member of one of the search parties. The noises come again and some of the slug hunters chase after him. The slug's antennae sweep the air. One slug pauses, its antenna twitch, turning in my direction, its head following. I freeze, holding my breath, not daring to move a muscle. The rest move on, chasing my crew mate. The rider of the slug in front of me makes a noise, It's a weird noise, part growl, part chitter. My gaze creeps upwards, the slug is huge, a yellow colour, its skin has hard scales protecting it. The rider has two legs on this side of the slug, in some kind of saddle and a pair of arms holding some kind of reins around the slug's head. Some kind of wings are flared out behind it and a spider-like abdomen rests on the back of the slug. My look reaches the head. Its antenna are pointed in my direction and its huge spider-like eyes seem fixed upon me. I gulp in air, praying that this pair hasn't actually found me, when a human scream fills the air.

My head shoots around in the direction of the cries and the slug moves off towards them. Cold sweat runs down my back, I have never felt so terrified. Horrible ripping noises come from the slope as I gingerly creep forwards. When I get to the edge of the shade and look down, I swallow back the bile filling my mouth. Shards of red flesh are splattered across the ground and the slugs are slurping on bones. The insects are piling chunks of flesh in baskets and separating the organs, a pile of skins and entrails are off to one side. A head sits in a gold basin, as I watch they place the heart next to it and a large green insect moves forward, picks up the basin and moves away with it.

Another group of slugs arrive, they unload cocoons from the backs of the slugs and carry them towards this abattoir, laying them in a line. A red insect comes up and slices them open. It's the members of one of the search parties, they appear to be unconscious or paralysed. The insect examines them and points to two. The other insects grab the rest and carry them to the far side of this space. If I squint hard I can make out something that looks like a set of cages, my crew mates are shoved in, the doors closed and left. The red insect is inspecting the two men left, they are twitching and possibly waking up. I don't want to see what I think is going to happen next, but we have to know, if we are going to plan an escape.

Something rustles behind me and I swing around, it's that yellow slug. Its rider has dismounted and is standing next to me. Pain flares in my head as it grabs me and I hear a voice.

"Ah, such a strong mind for a mammal, so curious and inventive. Your breed will provide plenty of food for the hive, both as workers and as meat."

He makes a chittering noise and a response comes from behind me. I turn and see that the red insect has paused and that the two men are now being lifted and carried towards the cages. Blood is left on the ground.

"Those two are being retained as cattle as they are both healthy, since we can use the injured back as your base for the necessary biological investigations instead. Such a pity that you decided to follow the guadapa back to our hive, if you had stayed put then moonrise would have provided the water you need and we may not have found your people for many weeks. Instead you have given away your base and the other scouting party. Come, our queen will wish to test your latent psi talent before you are put with the rest of herd. You can explain their new future to them, that they are now workers, breeding stock and food for the hive."

80

Horror's Heart

Paul Edwards

Kincaid stared up at the decaying apartment complex, a mixture of dread, fear and something vaguely like hope coursing through his veins. *What I'd give to just slip into a state of emotional numbness,* he thought. He was so tired of feeling. Tired of this world and of himself, too.

He clenched and unclenched his hands. Pushed through the main communal door and entered the building.

Rubble, twisted pieces of metal and broken glass lay scattered across the floor. He edged around the debris, taking and climbing the stairs, wood clattering together in his backpack. He thought of the creature he was about to meet – the heart of the horror which had terrorised this city. How she might offer an alternative form of existence. Help him to forget the family he'd had. The crippling self-loathing that never went away…

He reached the top floor, gripped the handrail and paused momentarily for breath. A haunting piano riff playing alongside some achingly sad violins came from a room just along the corridor.

The door to that apartment stood ajar. Kincaid opened it wide, scanning the curios, ornaments and trinkets on display. An animal skull with twisting antlers. An abstract painting depicting two black holes leaking crimson paint. A goldfish bowl with a human skull inside. A large coffin, the lid raised, its interior lined with velvet.

The music was coming from an old-fashioned gramophone, its strange, repetitive melody echoing around and around inside his head. It had done its job of bringing him here, of leading him to her lair.

Stood at the window was the creature he was seeking, a tall and slender figure, a network of veins visible in her too-pale hands and face.

She glanced at him as he entered the room. "I was wondering when you were going to come."

Kincaid froze, his stony silence prompting her to turn around completely. His heart trembled. She was beautiful. Monstrous, too.

"I've been listening to all the shouting and cheering," she said. "Watching the marches and pyres being built. You've won, right? Just me left now." She tilted her head to one side. "You don't look capable of killing to me. How many have you slain, then?"

It took him a moment to find his voice. "Hundreds. Over a thousand, maybe."

She brushed back the midnight stream of her hair with both hands. "I'm their leader," she said, "and you've found me. You must be feeling pretty pleased with yourself."

"Doesn't the sun…?" He waved vaguely in the direction of the window.

She laughed and shook her head. "I won't go away. *Can't* go away. I am endless. Eternal."

He slid the backpack off his shoulder and put it down on the hard surface of the floor. "I've killed," he said, "just so I can get close to you. I want you all to myself." A smile tugged at his lips. "The Agency sent for me because I'm the best. Although I'm nothing like them. I'm as much an outsider as you are."

"Shouldn't you at least be wielding one of those right now?" She nodded at the pack between his feet.

"I hate what I am," he said, ignoring the comment. "Detest what I'm a part of. Feelings are such awful, shackling things."

"Pass me a stake," she said, sounding bored already.

Kincaid glanced down, shrugged and then unzipped his backpack. He pulled out a stake, straightened it and handed it to her. She gripped it in a deathly-white fist. Held it close to her chest, pressing the sharpened point to her heart. Her other hand grabbed it, too. Before he could say or do anything, she stabbed herself, thrusting the stake hard and deep into her chest, her face convulsing in a series of violent spasms.

He jolted forward, hands reaching out for nothing. Then her features relaxed. Her arms collapsed to her sides.

"Told you," she smiled. "Nothing can make me go away."

Her hands were on the stake again. He watched in disbelief as she slid it back out. It dropped and clattered to the floor.

Kincaid closed his eyes.

"I've wanted you for such a long time," he said. "Since it all began to fall apart. I don't care about any of it. My life. Them out there. Only you. I only ever think about you now."

The music stopped, the gramophone clicking still.

His eyelids lifted.

She was reaching for him with open arms.

He shuffled toward her, those arms snaking around his neck, her teeth swiftly finding the pulse point in his throat. A flash of pain – and then he was fading away from himself, throwing off the shackles, passing from one plane of existence to another.

The next thing he knew, he was sat propped upright on a chair. He lifted his head, noticing she'd drawn the curtains to block out the sunlight.

She was standing over him, grinning, her eyes big, black and wide.

He put his hand to his neck. Winced and then brought it away again. Blood glistened on his fingertips.

"We needn't be alone anymore," she whispered. "I'm the monster of your world, you're the horror of mine." She offered him her hand. "We were made for each other."

He gripped her fingers, rising to his full height. They made their way over to her bed. She laid inside it first, arms reaching for him again. He gazed down into her ashen face, those abyssal eyes...

"Now it starts over," she said. "We begin again."

He lowered himself into her embrace, her arms and legs wrapping around him, her mouth fastening on to his throat.

They might unleash a second plague, he thought. Become king and queen of some twisted, necrotic empire.

How do I feel, he wondered.

She reached up, grabbed hold of an ornate handle and pulled the coffin lid down. Nothing, he realised, devoured by darkness.

Finally, I feel nothing.

The Tooth Fairy

Rickey Rivers Jr.

1.

I keep a lot, but I'm not a hoarder. I just have a bunch of boxes. The boxes are for clothes and stuff, important stuff. I wanted to give the old clothes away, but I never got around to it. Sometimes you can't help but to keep old stuff, even if you don't need it anymore. My dad left me a record player and a box of old records. He was big into blues and jazz. I never got into that stuff. I like rock. I'd like to own a record store someday. There's a lot of money in nostalgia.

I've got several televisions, fat and flat. Some are color TVs, some are black and white and one in particular hums when you switch it on. It's a nice low hum. It's like hearing life fade every time you turn the knob. One day it won't work anymore. I barely watch anything, but I keep the TVs. They're memories.

***

I like radios. I have two, one from my mother and one from my father. My father's radio is a small one he had in the military. He carried it with him in his pocket from here to there and back. He said it kept him company when people couldn't. It takes batteries. I still have the same ones in there. I don't listen to his radio much.

Mom's radio is bigger. It plugs in. It's brown with a white panel and black dials. It works too. Sometimes I like to shut off all the lights and lie down on the floor with the radio on my favorite station. They play rock all day. At night there's a talk show with people who talk politics for a living. That seems like a nice job.

I don't understand politics. It seems dumb half the time. Mom never got into it, but Dad loved it. He used to talk about it with co-workers on the phone. Sometimes he'd get upset about what the president did or said. Mom said it was silly to get so worked up about things you couldn't change. But dad said it wasn't silly. He said it was silly to stop caring. He said it was silly to accept how things are.

"To accept is to die."

***

I have books, too. I like reading. I like waking up early and reading in the sunlight. "The natural light that shines on us all." Mom said that. She said a pastor said that once and it stuck with her. Now it's with me.

I have toys that still work, too and a box of old cards, some from birthdays, some from Christmas and other holidays. I like to read through them every so often. One time I found some money in one. It was five dollars and it fell out of a Father's Day card. Sometimes this box makes me happy, but other times the box makes me sad. I like the box. Memories fall out.

Speaking of, I also have a box of paper and plastic (receipts, driver's licenses). I put them in the same box. I don't have as many licenses as receipts but then again who does? I look into this box on occasion. I don't feel a lot from this box. Some of the receipts have made me laugh before but that was before. Now I see them as items and prices on paper and nothing more. I mean, that's all they are anyway. The line before the last line rhymed and I didn't plan that. That's fun.

***

I have a box of photos too. This box is fun. It has a lot of family and miscellaneous photos. Come to think of it, I never use the word 'miscellaneous' in actual speech. I usually say etcetera and now as I write 'etcetera' I think about not being used to typing that word out fully. Instead I use the first three letters like everyone else. Everyone seems similar. I guess I'm part of that group.

Sometimes I think the old licenses should be with the photo box because they're also photos, but then I change my mind. In relation to the family photos is also a box of VHS tapes. Some of the tapes are family videos. Years ago Dad bought a camcorder and filmed a bunch of stuff. I guess he thought we'd always go back and watch them. Sometimes I do. They're nice.

I forgot the brand name of the camcorder. I put it away in another box. In that box is the other tape he filmed for Mom. On that tape he's talking directly into the camcorder. In that tape he read something he wrote. He wanted Mom to watch it, but I didn't think she needed to. That box pretty much belongs to him.

Also in that box is a medal he won in high school. He used to wrestle. He wanted me to learn how but I never had interest. The medal is silver. It belongs in the box. This place is no place for second place.

2.

Rereading this back it sounds like I live surrounded by boxes, but that's not true. A lot of them are in the garage. They're neatly put away so that getting through the garage isn't hard. You just have to walk through a maze. Sometimes I think that I keep too much stuff, but then I rethink that. Thoughts hurt sometimes.

That reminds me of a special non-boxed item. My Mom gave me a small white and gold toy treasure chest. Well, it's ceramic. So it's not really a toy. You'd have to see it. I thought it was pretty. Inside she kept my baby teeth. I still have it. The teeth are still in there. I don't know what to do with them. Sometimes I wonder why the tooth fairy never came to get them. I guess she didn't want them. I counted the teeth before and it came out to forty seven. It's much more now. If the tooth fairy paid a dollar for every tooth I'd be close to rich, richer really, because you can't outweigh the spirit. Mom said that.

I remember one time I thought the tooth fairy did come for my teeth. I saw her with Dad. I remember being happy to see the tooth fairy for the first time. I was gonna tell everyone at school that I finally saw her. I was gonna ask for an autograph. But that wasn't her. That was only a woman.

***

A thought came to mind, something about the song "I Saw Mommy Kissing Santa Claus." I never saw Dad be Santa. Dad never wanted to be. Dad never wanted to be a father. And Mom never wanted to dress like a fictional character. Mom wanted to be Mom, a mother. I guess we all grow and see how lies can lead to pain.

The tooth fairy wasn't real. She was a woman like any other and she flew into our home that night. I was supposed to be asleep. Mom was supposed to be gone. But I saw what I saw and I recorded it. And that's why Mom couldn't see the tape Dad wanted her to see. His apology couldn't fix anything. It couldn't make any fantasy of a happy home real. The only way that fantasy could be real is if he was out of the home. He could live with his fantasy away from us.

Every tooth I have is a separate wish and I've always made the same wish. Even if every tooth wasn't mine, it didn't matter and it shouldn't matter to a fictional fairy.

***

It's sad when people go away in a box. I cried a lot at Mom's funeral. I didn't know how to move on. Dad's funeral was different. I didn't want to go in the first place. I wanted to spit on the box he was in, but I wasn't brave enough to do it. Mom stood by me, clutching my hand. She was crying like she didn't know what he did to her, like she didn't know how much pain he had caused her by kissing on some woman in a little girl's dress.

I sometimes wish Mom had been smarter, if she were she wouldn't have taken him back the first time. After the first cheat it's not like it stops. And it really didn't stop for Dad. Every tooth fairy had a different look and they were all different compared to Mom. None of those women meant anything to Dad. They were distractions. I see that now. He was so brave to bring one into the house.

I'm not sure if he ever really loved Mom. He might have only loved her enough to have me. Maybe he was cheating in the army too? Some people say taking large amounts of time away from your wife to do anything else is just like cheating. So I guess the time away from us was cheating all along. He didn't deserve mom. She was a good woman, and good women get hurt.

I had to hurt some women, but they weren't good. They were only as good as their teeth. The only use for teeth outside of a mouth is using them for wishes. If kisses were wishes Dad would be rich, but he wasn't rich. He could never be rich. He could only be dead in a box.

Joy

SJ Townend

It's the things we don't *have* to do which we enjoy most, isn't it?

Puddings, the first whisky after sundown, behaving chivalrously; pleasure hatches where nothing is expected of us.

George Farrington, a sculpted beast of a boy, came from a background of privilege yet found joy—true feverish passion—in little. Despite his cemented neutrality and shoulder-shrugging disinterest in the world around him, he excelled at everything he did. He was one of those grating children who became one of those annoying teenagers: effortlessly handsome, the fastest rower, top of every class—yet his eyes carried no flame for life. His body was a cold hearth full of cinder; ash left from a fire that no-one had witnessed.

He was not depressed as such, for how could one be down when one suffers no emotional ebb and flow, no fluctuation? He was simply a flat ocean, a fisherman's dream, a permanent state of insensibility. Farrington had cashed in his chips at birth to spend life waiting for a boat that would never arrive to carry him to a timeless destination whilst the world blew hurriedly around him. Life felt to him like a balled chore bashing at his shins; pointless. Too unperturbed to kick it away, he tolerated existence.

Not even freedom from the mundane, prescriptive education that adulthood delivered brought him joy.

Whilst knee-high to a high-knee and undoubtedly a tedium draped around calves and heels, Ma and Pa—his parents, wealthy sorts—parcelled him off to a city centre boarding school. In character, he went without fuss, caring not for the kiss goodbye his mother planted nor the stuffed bear his father gifted. Days, weeks, months, a term passed as knowledge and sport, sport and knowledge sunk in via osmotic exposure. He didn't look forward to returning home to see his family for the holidays and did not care where he spent his vacation period. He would just have readily spent summer alone in the woods of his parents' estate, trapping pheasants, as at school with the skeletal holiday staff, strolling the pavements each day until term recommenced, surrounded by city strangers with whom he did not have to interact, kicking stones and pigeons. It wasn't that people brought him displeasure, or the eyes of others pricked at his skin, he just didn't care for folk.

He received a good schooling— measurably the best—and his knowledge of the world, of science, history and mathematics was second to none. Unceremoniously, he found himself shuttled down the corridor of education, propelled forwards by the harping hands of time and overpaid staff, towards something he still felt nothing for.

He plummeted unaware from his birth nest, collecting qualifications like the slow creep of middle-aged spread which gathers without notice along the way until one's trousers simply fit no more, he did not feel the pull of gravity tugging him earthwards down, towards adulthood. Of course, he aced medical school with minimal effort whilst coincidentally sleeping his way through the undergraduate catalogue— persuaded by many, chasing none— and ended up specialising in cardiothoracic surgery at the most prestigious hospital in the west. It was as if one day, as the bird fell, he simply awoke, scalpel in hand.

Day in, day out, the earth span on its stick as Farrington cut, cracked and splayed ribs with mechanical precision; his fingers plumed and stitched defunct vessels and gave first class people a second chance at life. A surgeon he was, a surgeon he had become. Some nine hundred patients he'd saved by the end of his first year in practice—never a patient lost on his table was. He'd have kept a personal tally—if he'd cared. It paid the bills, kept blue fillet steak on the table, gave him reason enough to move his meat each day.

One evening, after a day that had been just like all the others, whilst walking the diagonal to his penthouse through the city park under the linear arch of tipped trees, each tickling its opposing partner's canopy, he heard a bird—a sparrow— lying under a red maple.

What beauty.

Fallen from its roost? Dropped by a hunter? He stooped to look down at the thing of insignificance all-a-twitch by his boot. He watched its tiny chest rise and fall and rise and fall, staccato, an oscillating spring undoubtedly coming soon to rest. Both wings were twisted, bent from how they were happy to be and a vermillion rivulet of fresh blood seeped: a slow balloon of red inflating on the path. Injured, its eyes still shone more life than his ever had—

Until he lifted up his colossal foot and brought it down on the bird. Down hard and fast and meteorically; crater-inducing, sudden.

Crunch.

Snap.

The bird, quashed and as flat as his temperament had been until this day, now took on its angelic wings. Its soul rose heavenwards, a gory residue of cherry-grey tissue still smeared on the path now lifeless left.

George cleaned his booted foot where grass tufts hugged an edge of cement and walked onwards, back towards his pad with pace. A tingle in the pit of his stomach spread swiftly to his fingers and toes. An internal glow spread torso to limb like the rolling in of a high tide awash with firefly shrimp, each wave crest spilling with hundreds flicking their lights on and off, wriggling and writhing and pushed sandwards, shrimpwrecked, desperate to breed. An orgasmic feeling, a serotonin celebration exploded in his heart: a ticket with six matching numbers, a thousand candles all lit at once, euphoria.

He could suddenly smell the sunshine.

Joy.

Joy struck, crashing into the walls of his chest as if a million sparrows had taken flight within its containment. Heady emotions capriciously flooded the shadowy citadel walls of his constitution. No longer flat, his joy bled into the three dimensional world, smacked and lifted as if served with a true love's first kiss.

Farrington operated the next day, but, onwards, his track record of unmitigated success slipped fast.

Best Be Ware

Rie Sheridan Rose

The marrow bones
rattle
in the wind
tonight—

and on the
vast moor,
something howls...

They say the
Hunt
will ride
tonight—

searching for
souls
to harvest
like grapes.

Best be ware
and lock
the bairns
in the cupboards.

'Tis an
evil wind
that carries

the cry of
the horn

and
all heads
turn
when the
Hunt
rides by.

Visitor

Rickey Rivers Jr.

1.

[Voice of Anna J. Lee (Mother of Jamie Quinn Lee)]

"I remember her telling us about the experience several times. I just didn't know what to do or how to deal with it. How can any parent?

"I've never been through anything like that, but she had been so detailed about it I knew she couldn't be lying. She was scared. Then when the encounters advanced to a sexual nature, I was just... Sometimes, you just don't know what to do.

"Our pastor prayed over the room and the entire house but she was still visited. We tried to help her as best we could. Counseling came next. We certainly didn't want to put her on medication. She was just a young girl. What could I have done?"

***

[Voice of William Lee (Father of Jamie Quinn Lee)]

"It's terrible thing to hear, your little girl going through that. She came to us and laid the situation out plain. You could tell she'd been crying.

"My first thought was to go to her school. I thought she was speaking in code, trying to let us know it was one of the teachers or boys at school, but she made it clearer-this was a home invasion. Though not an invasion of our home, the visitor only came to her.

"She spoke so vividly about the visits. When she left, she called us and said the encounters worsened. The things she told me. [Exhales] I can't repeat, but she suffered and I hate to say that. You don't want your child to suffer."

***

[Voice of Karen Cooper (Friend of Jamie Quinn Lee)]

"No, she wasn't always like that. We did normal stuff together. Hanging out, going to parties, talking about boys, sleepovers, you know. That was so long ago, though.

"She only started mentioning nightmares after one of the sleepovers. The next morning, she came up to me crying and asking me why I didn't wake up. She said she was trying to get me to help her but I didn't know what she was talking about. Apparently, the previous night she'd been visited and struggled to get my attention. I thought she was making it up. I didn't know what was going on with her. I only found out later that she had been molested. The story was a supposed "night visitor," that no one else could see had been the culprit. Honestly, I took her less and less seriously."

2.

[The following voices are of James Benjamin (Journalist) and Strawberry Jane (occupation withheld)]

JB: "Did you know Jamie Quinn?" [Picture presented]

SJ: "Yeah, I knew her."

"At that time, did she ever mention anything about having… strange dreams?"

"Sure, but they were only dreams."

"Why do you say that?"

"Many of the girls who work here have been molested. Some of them get creative with how it happencd."

"Did she call it that, molestation?"

"No, she tried to deny it. Tried to convince folks about what happened. Night terrors, I told her- or nightmares, whatever."

"You didn't want to believe her?"

"I didn't say that. You could tell something happened. The look-you could see it in her eyes. The girl was troubled. Then again, plenty of us are. [Laughs] But she looked a different kind of troubled, the kind where you could tell she didn't sleep at night. The kind where you could tell it wouldn't be long before she went all the way loopy."

"All the way loopy?"

"Insane, come on slick, you know what I mean."

"Right and had any of the other girls had similar stories?"

"None like hers."

"Have you spoken to her lately?"

"I haven't seen that child in a long time. I don't know what happened to her."

"Did she seem to be scared?"

"She looked scared all the time, like a rookie, but different. She wasn't scared of the men. She told me she was scared to go to sleep. She wanted to always be awake. She said sleeping was the scariest part of being alive."

"Do you believe that?"

"I believe that she believes it. As for me, I sleep well after working. I don't have those problems."

"Lucky you!"

"Yeah, lucky me, ha! I guess you can say that. Now, pay up. Same price no matter what didn't happen."

"I have more questions."

[Sighs] "Go on."

"Did she describe any of the encounters to you?"

"Yeah, but they were the loopy versions. She talked about staring up at the ceiling, her door opening and someone rubbing her legs in the dark and then it leading to sex. Just normal stuff."

"Normal stuff?"

"Normal around here, except we can see who's doing it- [laughs]. Sometimes they don't want to be seen, though."

"What do you mean by 'seeing who's doing it?'"

"We can see the men we're sleeping with. Jamie Quinn was talking like the man was invisible."

"So, she did say man?"

102

"No, I say man. She said the person spoke unisex-whatever that means. Said they were real gentle with her until they weren't. Sounds like some of the guys around here. They put on the act of being shy and then they want to manhandle you and that's when you teach them a lesson. Like I said, some of the girls get creative with their stories. Plenty of us been touched before graduation, you understand?"

"Yes, I understand. Did that happen to you?"

[Exhales loudly] "I thought you wanted information on Jamie Quinn? You said you weren't a cop, was that a lie?"

"Oh no, not a lie."

"Then don't ask questions about me."

"I'm sorry. Do you have any more information that might be useful?"

"I don't think so. She was interesting. Like I said, you can tell when one's gone all the way, creative type.

"Do you think there's any truth to her stories?"

"I believe that something happened. I'm just not sure it happened the way she said. We all find ways to cope, hell-some of us force ourselves to forget. Some of us make up scenarios. Some of us try and can't forget and end up running, like her, but you can't run from problems forever. Eventually, you look back and see those problems are still there. Now, let's say I believed her. Do you actually think it's possible to run away from sleep? How long could you run?"

"Until you were tired enough to stop running."

"Exactly. We need sleep. Even after a long night that girl still didn't sleep. She told me. You should have seen how she looked. Her face told you the whole scene."

"What did her face tell you?"

"Everything, -She'd been through a lot. Not unusual around here but the look in her eyes was different. That chick used to freak me out with some of those stories. Sometimes I wanted to shake her. She scared the other girls. Whatever happened to her was at least real enough in her mind. And when it's real in your mind… it's real enough to scare you. Like I said, we all cope. You just gotta separate that fiction from reality."

"There can be truth in fiction."

"Sure, truth is stranger than fiction. Maybe I've been living in reality too long to believe it, though. The reality here is things like that don't happen. No invisible visitors, just people who take advantage of folks."

"Do you believe in sleep paralysis?"

"Yeah, that's not fiction. I've had that."

"And you believe in molestation. So, isn't it plausible that both can combine?"

"Sure but… not in that way. The way she described it was… [she wraps her arms around herself] too terrible to believe."

"So, you didn't want to believe all of what she said?"

"I couldn't, why would I believe something like that? Matter of fact, why are you asking so many questions about her? Is she okay?"

104

3.

[Handwritten by Jamie Quinn Lee] (Recovered)

Don't think of it as a dream. It happened. I was thirteen, lying in bed, asleep, but not at the same time. I was awake, but not at the same time. My body was stiff, I couldn't move. I was conscious. I could move my eyes but not my head. My mouth could open and close but not to say words, only to make a weak sound like a baby. I could produce tears, involuntarily or otherwise. I'd get scared enough to just cry, wide open eyed tears.

Later, I learned this to be sleep paralysis. Many people have experienced sleep paralysis and some have told tales of being watched by shadow people. They may be tales but I don't doubt their claims. Some have said they've experienced pain even after waking. I wish that was all for me.

"I didn't see shadow people, I didn't see anyone. There was no pain, not at first. The first time I just couldn't move. The next time was at fourteen. I couldn't talk or move. This time the door to my bedroom opened. I'd been facing away from the door so I only heard the sound of it creaking open. I knew it wasn't a shadow person because I could clearly hear approaching footsteps. This person came to my bed and stood over me for a time. I couldn't see their face. I strained my eyes, there was only darkness. Soon I felt a hand against my foot through the covers. The hand went up my leg and stopped. Then the motion repeated, from foot to leg over and over again. It felt like they were stroking me like a cat. I woke up and my door was closed. The room was dark and quiet.

This has happened several times in the past few years. At one point the stroking went from foot up to my head. Again, I could feel everything. Again, I couldn't move. Another time my sheets were pulled off and I could feel two hands touching me, rubbing me. And another time still I felt the bed shifting, like someone had climbed in. I could feel them sniff my hair and skin-then just lie there until I woke up.

This was a person. It couldn't have been a shadow person. I felt everything this person did to me. I want to make that clear. It took so long to work up the courage to tell my parents. It hurt when at first I could tell they didn't believe me. Finally, my dad put a lock on my door and told me to keep it locked when I slept. The lock did nothing.

These are not hallucinations, though I wish they were. You don't know what it's like to feel those hands on you, human-like hands. I don't know what to officially call it. Be it demon or entity. I feel like I shouldn't give it a name.

***

[Handwritten by Jamie Quinn Lee] (Recovered)
Now that I live alone, I've done the following: Slept in different rooms besides my bedroom. Double and triple checked the locks on my doors every night before bed. When sleep I keep a weight (twenty pounds) balanced against my bedroom door to wake me just in case. I've watched my diet, cut

106

back on sugars and caffeine. I've taken fewer showers and baths. I've urinated on myself from time to time as a precaution. I want to be unclean. I've hung up dreamcatchers as well.

All of this has been to no avail. The visits have continued, now more aggressive, as if the visitor is angry. They've advanced to intercourse-painful intercourse. I'm sure the visitor is upset.

4.

[Handwritten by James Benjamin (Journalist)]

It is an unornate truth that they may never find her. Yet still the truest possibility beyond fiction. Fiction is funny. And some still don't believe the tale, as if such truth can't possibly exist in this life, in this world.

I believe the girl. I have had too many dead-end interviews leading to the same conclusion. And that is the fact that no one truly knows but her. Those who know her only know slivers of the truth. Like a pie, the pieces add up to a whole. I believe she remains among the now and the after, a body made astral through apparitional intercourse. Some say different, as if to blame the girl. But blaming the girl is wrong.

I wish we had a trace of her to go on beyond writing-, a limb, a nose, a bloody clump of hair, anything at all. At least that would confirm the abduction took place. Neither confirming nor denying to the parents is terrible. In that regard I don't envy the police. "I don't know," is such a terrifying answer to someone seeking solace. And yet that is all anyone has.

I feel for the girl. I feel for the parents, for the public. I feel for their sanity, much less my own. Wrapping your head around the existence of the girl's descriptions makes me afraid to fall asleep. I do sleep, of course, but it is terribly unwell.

I think about her as if she'd reveal universal truths to me. I lay there in my lonely home and pray in the dark. I wonder if I'll ever wake up frozen-, if I'll ever feel hands on my legs-, if I'll ever leave this world conscious of transport.

I wonder a lot lying there, how afraid she must have been, how afraid I am by the simple idea of lacking a straight solution to something so fantastic.

Hair of the Dog

Chris Rodriguez

Rigo pushed at the bed covers stuck against his sticky body. No breeze infiltrated the screen on the open window. The night air hung still and heavy. The near full moon threw a bright, burning light across his bare skin.

"He's having those dreams again, Carlos," he heard his mother say from the next room.

"The ones where he's the monster?" his father grunted in frustration.

"Yes. I'm afraid of what's going on with that boy."

Rigo squirmed. He dreaded what was coming next. Same conversation every time the dreams started up.

"It's puberty. Hormones going nuts. I know he sprouted some hair this summer."

"He's only 12!" His mother clearly didn't think his father was on the right track.

Rigo didn't know for sure if it was normal, but hair was growing on his body. Hair in places even the older boys didn't have. Strange coarse hair on his head forming a Mohawk-type crown ran down the back of his neck. This unruly broom refused to lie down no matter what his mother or barber did. Other weird stuff, too. His fingernails were thick and coarse for a little boy.

When he went for his annual physical, Dr. Berry had told his mother, it wasn't unusual. Some people often have thicker nails and Rigo's had no color change or indicators of bad health. That and the new growth of hair was nothing to be worried about, he assured her. He took a sample of Rigo's blood to check for anomalies. Normally, the sight of a needle would have been enough to send Rigo screaming from the room, but right now he was much more afraid of what was happening to his body, normal or not.

He untangled gangly limbs from the cloying sheets, slid off the bed and shoved his feet into the new slippers, remembering the conversation with his mother about them.

"Rigo! I just bought new clothes and shoes for you at the beginning of summer. You can't have grown so fast."

He had reluctantly removed his socks and showed her how long his toes had grown. Now, a few weeks later, they were so long the toe joints were starting to bend upward. He didn't dare tell his mother he might need new shoes again soon.

"That boy is growing much too fast, Alicia," his father chimed in. He puffed out his chest with pride and grinned.

Rigo could see his father was not in the least concerned about the strange things happening to his son's body. He had always been small for his age. Both parents were small, like so many people in the Mexican/American border town. His grandfather told him they came from tough Indian stock. When they moved across the border to Texas so his father

110

could work for a local rancher, he wasn't able to see his grandfather as often. Rigo had loved listening to the old stories about his ancestors. Even the scary ones about mythical creatures or animal spirits. Carlo's father was a kind and entertaining man. Everyone in his village loved him.

At the physical exam, Dr. Berry had asked, "Any odd genetic traits in your family I need to know about?"

Rigo's mother avoided Dr. Berry's eyes and seemed to be searching her memory. "No." she shrugged her shoulders.

"No cancer, diabetes or other disease, especially in your parents?"

Alicia again avoided the doctor's inquiring eyes. "My mother was never sick a day in her life. She still works."

"And your father?"

Rigo noticed his mother squirm uncomfortably. He had never heard about his maternal grandfather. She had never mentioned him to Rigo. Now he was curious. He turned to watch his mother's response to the probing question.

"I don't know anything about my father," Alicia finally admitted. "He was shot and killed when I was very young."

Rigo wondered why his grandfather had been shot. Had he been drunk, like so many men from his mother's village where they couldn't find work? Had he been stealing food for his family? It was no use wondering and he instinctively understood his mother did not want to talk about it.

111

He quietly opened his bedroom door and peeked into the hallway. They had a large house out on the edge of town. Usually, families like his were crowded into small migrant sheds or apartments in town, depending on where they were able to get jobs. He was the only child in his family so three people rattled around in the old farmhouse situated near the ranch where his father worked as a mechanic. He padded to the kitchen with the floorboards emitting the inevitable creak and squeak. His parents worked hard and slept hard. He could hear Carlos' soft snore as he reached the refrigerator.

Rigo's stomach was roaring for no reason. He had eaten every bite of his mother's Friday night special. She tended to cook the same thing every week so she didn't have to spend time planning meals and shopping. Rigo had heard his father tell people, "Alicia is not the greatest cook, but provides us with large healthy meals. We can't complain."

Tonight's meal had been one of Rigo's personal favorites. Arroz con Pollo served with the usual pinto beans, this time with fresh chopped tomato and cilantro from his mother's small garden and warm fresh tortillas on the side. He had two helpings and was going for a third when his mother put her hand over his reaching fingers so his father could take the last piece of chicken from the bowl.

"What has gotten into you, Rigo?" his mother had inquired.

"Leave him alone," Carlos said. "He's a growing boy."

"Carlos, he'll get sick if he keeps eating so much."

Rigo didn't realize how much he had eaten. He was embarrassed about it now and even more ashamed to be sneaking into the kitchen to see what else might be available to munch on. Nothing, no leftovers and the family did not snack, like many others.

He trudged back to his room, telling his growling stomach it would have to wait until morning. In reply, his belly let out a long, discontented growl. "Hey, I don't want to be fat like Juan Gonzalez," he answered it back. Juan was an unfortunate boy in his school. Everyone teased him. Rigo sympathized, but Juan also had bad gas and made the stinky, as his mother called it. He smelled so bad nobody could get close enough to make friends. Maybe the cruel kids at school would be giving Juan a break since Rigo was sure they would be making fun of his weird hair soon.

Rigo climbed back into bed, pushing the sodden sheets away from his feverish body. The incandescent moon had traveled higher. It no longer burned directly on his overheated body. He closed his eyes to try to sleep. Swift lights and shadows across his sensitive eyelids made him flinch and jerk, but soon he fell into a fitful dream state.

Rigo floated in the air, high enough to see trees below. He lazily flapped his long wings once, twice to stay in the thermal lift emanating off the hot desert floor. It was dark, but the bright moon lit the landscape below. A movement on the ground caught his eye as a lone rabbit emerged with caution from the den nestled under small boulders at the foot of a hill. Rigo watched it venture further from the entrance to nibble on the tender vegetation nearby. He scanned the landscape for other intruders and when none were located, he folded his wings and dove down like a bullet toward the unsuspecting prey. At the last second, he threw out his wings like brakes at the same time his legs dropped down from where they had been tucked tight into his body. His talons stretched forward and SWOOP!, grabbed the rabbit effortlessly before lifting it off the ground with a few powerful flaps of his long wings.

A large oak tree offered a perfect horizontal branch to perch. The rabbit was still. Rigo's razor talons had severed the tiny vertebrae. Even so, the rabbit still breathed, the heartbeat strong and rapid. The body was warm and Rigo could smell the blood coming from the fresh wound. He bent his head and tore the fur away to expose skin, then stripped shreds of meat off the bones to get to the tender parts inside. The prey's eyes watched the hunter's every move, still alive for far too long.

Rigo woke in a sweat and thrashed around in bed until he was sitting straight up. Breath rasped in his panic-constricted chest. He pushed the coarse hair down on his head and scrubbed at his crusty eyes, trying to focus. The old clock radio read 6:09 a.m. He reached over to turn it off so it wouldn't click on in 20 minutes. He wasn't in the mood for the golden oldies. Rigo heard his parents chatting over coffee and smelled the bacon, beans and

114

potatoes his mother fried up for breakfast. Barefooted, he shuffled to the bathroom and looked in the mirror.

What the hell was that dream all about? He'd dreamed a lot lately, worse than this one. It wasn't the first time he had killed in his sleep. *Why am I having them?* He wondered if it was the higher levels of testosterone Dr. Berry had mentioned. Whatever testosterone was, he didn't want it in his body if it made him feel so strange.

The mirror did not register what Rigo expected. He saw no major changes in his appearance. At least no *new* changes. The unruly shock of the mohawk mane stuck up above his head. He sighed and reached in the drawer for scissors to trim it back down to the crown where his "normal" hair would mostly cover it up. Then he shed his hair-itchy pajamas to get into the shower. He stopped dead. His heart beat like an oil pump in his chest as he pulled a black feather from under his arm.

Wait. It couldn't... What the hell?

He turned around in the mirror, checking the rest of his body. Rigo might have thought it was just something stuck in his pajamas except he had to pluck the feather from his skin, causing a distinct "pinch" where it was pulled and a small spot of blood. His mind in turmoil, he jumped into the shower and scrubbed every inch of his body until he tingled.

"Don't you want breakfast?" his mother said as he rushed out the door to head for school. "I'm not hungry," he said, tossing a wave goodbye above his head. He heard his parents no doubt discussing this first-time oddity as he jogged down the dirt drive to the main road where he would catch the bus.

Time at school dragged into what seemed like day-long hours. Rigo kept to himself as much as possible. He needed time to think. He took a seat under a skimpy tree in the corner of the grounds at lunch and watched the other 6th grade guys do what they always did, strut around being the undisputed top of the dogpile, flirting with girls, picking on boys who "didn't have what it took" to be in the popular groups. Usually he was the first to join in, to avoid being a victim himself.

Rigo agonized over the new hair growth on his body. It was normal, even for some guys his age, but he had seen other boys, older boys, at the pool and their hair was different. The hair on Rigo's body was coarse and wiry. It poked at him in tender places, making him writhe in discomfort. Adults were constantly telling him to sit still and quit squirming. His father had lots of dark hair all over his body. His mother teased Carlos all the time about looking and sometimes smelling, like an old goat. *Am I different? Is this really normal?*

"Hey, *pendejo*!" Someone kicked at his foot. "What do you think you're doing out here?"

The ugly mug glaring down would have scared him if it hadn't belonged to his best friend since kindergarten. "Just thinking. I haven't been feeling well," he confessed to Henry Beezus.

Henry's bright red hair was pulled back and tied with leather cord. His pale skin made his freckles pop like red prickly pear blossoms against the desert sand. When he and Rigo were small, they

116

were picked on regularly. Then Henry shot up a head above all the other boys the summer before 5th grade. Nobody picked on him anymore. They all called him Henry BeJeezus.

"What the hell do you have to think about?" Henry said as he plopped down beside his friend. "You in love?" He winked.

Rigo snorted. "That'll be the day." He could talk to Henry about anything, but this was different. "I'm not sleeping well. Nightmares. And," he blurted, "I've got hair growing in weird places. Even my mother's worried. She took me to a doctor!"

Henry put his head back on the tree and took a deep breath. "Yeah, I know what you mean, man. I started getting hair down there and under my arms last year. It's *so* weird! Itches like crazy. And my mom makes me wear deodorant now." He put a thick hand on Rigo's shoulder. "Don't worry. It happens to all of us. We're *men* now, dude!" He jumped up, swiped at the dust on the seat of his jeans and walked toward the building. The bell had rung to come back to class.

After school, Rigo dragged his feet up the lane, kicking fine dust. It settled on his pant legs and sneakers. He stomped them clean before entering the side of the house. The front door was only for company. They rarely had company clear out here. The screen door slammed behind him after letting a half dozen flies into the hot and aromatic kitchen. Mama had been baking.

117

"*Hijo*," I need to talk to you." She pulled a chair from under the worn kitchen table. "Look what I made." She slid a small plate of Mexican wedding cookies, his favorite and a tall glass of milk in front of him. They would have been wolfed down in a hot minute if he didn't have a flutter in his stomach reminding him of the dark wings in his dream.

"What's the occasion?" he said. "A party somewhere?" She only made them for special events in the town, never just for Rigo.

Alicia pulled out the chair next to him and dragged it a little closer. She sat, leaning nearer to her son. "Your father and I have talked and we've made a very difficult decision."

Now she had Rigo's attention. The last "difficult" decision they had made was when they put down the dog he'd known since birth. Rascal had fallen into an old well. All of his legs had been broken and he was eight years old. So was Rigo. They couldn't afford the medical attention or time it would take for the mutt to heal enough to walk, *if* he could ever walk again. Carlos took Rascal out to the ranch and he never came back. They didn't talk about it afterward. Rigo was young, not dumb.

"What is it, Mama?" His brow furrowed deep with worry. His hand shook as he reached for one of the cookies he couldn't bring to his mouth. Powdered sugar coated his brown, trembling fingers and fell like snow onto the tabletop. Saliva pooled in the back of his throat like it sometimes did before he vomited.

118

Alicia tried to smile, to show him it wasn't serious. The gesture failed to comfort him. "It's nothing, really. We think it is time you met my mother, your *Abuela* Maria."

His head swiveled toward her as he gazed deep into her eyes. "What? Why do you want me to meet her now? At the start of the school year?" He had a million questions. His reeling mind couldn't grasp the situation.

In twelve years, his mother had only mentioned her mother a few times and never suggested a visit. He was told his grandmother Maria lived in Mexico, far west of the Texas border, south of Arizona in a predominantly Yaqui village. He had heard his mother say the people there were very religious and attended the ancient adobe Catholic church daily. Rigo had been to many a Mass but his parents generally attended only the more important services. They both worked on Sundays. He didn't really know much more about Maria, other than her husband had apparently been killed as his mother had told Dr. Berry.

"It's just time," Alicia said quietly.

The words, the tone in his mother's voice chilled him to the bone. "Can I ask you a question?" He was careful as he had often been told children didn't need to know everything. It was considered rude. He always figured if he needed to know something, his parents would tell him.

She licked her lips, brow furrowed. "Yes. You may not get the answers you want to hear. Only the ones I can give you now."

"I heard what you told Dr. Berry about your father. What happened to him? Why have you never mentioned it before?"

"Rigo, I was just a little girl. Four years old. Even though I saw it happen, I didn't understand and my mother would never discuss it with me." She wrung her hands together. "Later when I was a older, *mi tio*, Juan-Carlo told me the story of what happened that night. I was confused. It didn't sound exactly like I remembered."

"What did you remember?" Rigo prompted her to continue.

"I was just a little girl, Rigo, I couldn't understand."

She took a deep breath and went inside herself, dredging the images from her memory from so long ago. "It was night-time. A noise woke me. I could hear my mother screaming outside. I was afraid and alone. When I went to the window, I saw my mother across the yard in the goat pen. She was screaming and waving the big gun, the shotgun. My mother screamed again as one of the goats was lifted into the air and thrown at her. Then the gun boomed so loud I covered my ears and squished my eyes shut. I was so afraid, I made water on the floor and slid down to sit and wait for someone to come comfort me. I called for my Papa, but he didn't come."

His mother was shaking hard and Rigo took her hand. "I'm sorry, Mother. Where was your father?"

She wiped her dripping eyes with her apron. "It seemed I sat on the wet floor for an eternity. My mother came back alone. She carried me to the bed where she rocked me until I went to sleep. In the morning, many men came and I saw them carry my father to a wagon and lay him down inside. They drove away quickly so I asked Mama why they were taking him. She said they were going to prepare his body to meet Jesus. She didn't talk about him again."

Rigo took it all in. "Then what did your uncle tell you that made you think his story was different?"

"He told me my father was a hero who had been shot by a thief trying to steal our goats. It happened all the time so I had no reason to think he was lying, however, the vision of my mother holding the gun and the sound it made going off didn't fit with his story."

Rigo's eyebrows shot up. "You think your mother shot your father?"

Alicia shrugged. "I was just a little girl. What did I know?"

Later that night, Rigo dreamed again.

Alarico Ibarra, known to the locals as El Zopalote, stood on the corner in front of the The Suds Bucket Bar puffing on a cigarette. If anyone dared look for Alarico, he could always be found there, day or night. It seemed he never slept. He looked uninterested in the world around him, but missed nothing through his heavily hooded eyes. He was dangerous. The locals guessed he worked for one of the big cartels, possibly Barrio Azteca. Nobody Rigo knew had ever asked.

The hair on Rigo's head bristled when Alarico dropped the spent butt, mashed it under his silver studded boot and walked toward the alley where Rigo was squatting in the shadows, watching and waiting. The man was not aware of his presence. Alarico went directly toward the trash bin, turned his back to the street and unzipped the distressed jeans clad in black leather motorcycle chaps.

As the abundant stream of piss washed over the back wall, Rigo crept from the shadows, slow padded steps, no sound from his large paws. He licked his lips in nervous anticipation and before the man could tuck himself back into his jeans, Rigo's powerful hind legs pushed against the pavement. He sprang into the air above the man.

Alarico instinctively spun around, pulling his weapon from the well-worn sheath on his leg. The bone-handled Schrade steelpoint glinted in the streetlight. It had killed and wounded many men and fucked up the faces of any woman who disobeyed him. He held it down low in a tight fist, ready to plunge up and out to gut the belly of whoever dared to mess with him. Alarico's eyes went wide in shock as his mind bent at the sight of the creature looming over him. He was slow in his reaction and the knife was knocked from his shaking hand, clattering to the ground harmless as a toothpick.

Rigo opened his slavering jaws wide as they came down over the man's bare head. The scream muffled as the skull caved between huge, jagged teeth. With blood and brains seeping into the back of his throat, Rigo gave the body hanging from his grizzled snout a quick shake. One massive hind leg with razor claws came forward to rake through the tough leather jacket gutting Alarico in one swift move. Loose, slimy intestines slid out in a steamy pile, plopping on the trash covered ground with a wet SMACK! A second later, the body dropped unceremoniously on top of them.

People inside the bar heard the commotion and crowded the sidewalk, then the entrance to the alley as they chattered, pointing at the unrecognizable pile of debris in the alley, the only thing left of a very bad man. Nobody called the police. All they saw was the shadow of the creature slinking away around the corner. It left behind a huge stinking pile of scat next to the dead man's body.

A high-pitched keening sound woke Rigo and sweat popped out on his forehead. He jumped out of bed, panting, the scream stifled deep in his throat. He shuffled out of his room, trying to get control of shaking extremities and became aware of a throbbing sting in his left hand. It was too dark in the hallway to see, but when he turned on the bathroom light, drops of blood dripped from the side of his palm. He grabbed a towel to wrap it.

Alicia came into the brightly lit room when she saw the door open. "What have you done, hijo?" she asked, grabbing his hand. The towel around it came loose and she saw the small gash on the edge.

"I – I don't know!" Rigo looked at his mother in horror. "I woke from this terrible dream and the wound was there."

His mother grabbed some bandages from a drawer and sat her son on the lid of the toilet. She cleaned and disinfected the wound, then covered it in gauze and tape. "You must not mention this to anyone," Alicia cautioned him. She grabbed his chin and looked directly into his eyes. "No one. You understand?"

He nodded, but in truth, did not understand.

"You go back to bed now. We will discuss this tomorrow." She gently guided him back into his bedroom and watched as he climbed back into bed. "Don't worry. We know what to do."

Rigo fought sleep. He lay awake, the dream playing over and over in his mind until his head pounded. In the morning, he got up and dressed as soon as he heard his mother in the kitchen.

"Your father has gone to the ranch to tell Senior Barrego we will be gone for a while." She continued to stir the oatmeal bubbling in the pot. "The people are talking. We can't wait any longer."

"What are they talking about?" Rigo asked, afraid to hear the answer. Alicia was silent. "Mama? Please tell me."

"A man was killed in town last night. A very bad man. Nobody cares about him, but what killed him has everyone fearing for their lives. They are talking about a creature, like a large dog. They have armed themselves with weapons to protect their families."

Rigo's head started pounding again. He was too afraid to ask more.

"We will leave immediately," his mother said. "Go and pack after you have eaten."

***

The drive to his grandmother's village was long and uneventful. Rigo had much to think about and plenty of time without interruption since his parents were not talking except about directions, where to eat, where to get fuel, etc. The first night they slept near the truck in the middle of nowhere. Carlos built a small campfire and they slept on blankets on the hard ground.

Roads were unpaved and dusty the last 50 miles or so and by evening Rigo spotted a small village at the base of a mountain dotted in chapparal and hardwoods. Snow blanketed the highest peak. A stream of clear water trickled down from the mountain to the tiny village where the people still used the large communal well to fill urns for use in the small adobe homes surrounding the plaza. A few people were out. Children played with sticks and balls as they ran and laughed between the crude structures. Women had started cooking fires in clay ovens and open pits. Men sat on benches talking together.

They turned to watch the old pickup as it rattled into town to stop at the side of Maria's small hut. A tiny, round woman came out to welcome them with open arms. Alicia ran to her as soon as the truck came to a stop.

The villagers stood and quietly watched the strangers as they greeted Maria. Then Rigo climbed down from the truck. He turned to look at the small crowds gathering as they pointed and whispered, obviously agitated at the appearance of this family. Rigo stood on the far side of the truck, feeling they were pointing at him, reluctant to move to his grandmother's side.

Three men who looked like priests walked through the gathering crowds, holding up hands to calm them. They smiled and nodded to the curious villagers clamoring to know who the intruders were. Rigo watched as they walked toward Maria's hut. Rigo joined his family wondering about the strange welcoming party.

His mother took his hand in hers. "It is time, Rigo. You will go with these men to the monastery." She turned to point to the large walled-in structure high up on the large mountain.

"They will keep you safe; help you control your power. Teach you everything you need to know."

"My power?" Rigo watched the men approach. Peace washed over his fevered body. His mother was right. He needed to go with these men. He was not afraid. This was what had to be done to keep him and others safe.

"Hello, Rigo," one of the priests said. "I am Father Antonio. I have known about you for a long time. Would you like to come with us?" He beamed a friendly smile. "We remember your grandfather. He was like you as a boy. Sadly, we could not hold on to him. We will teach you how to control your special powers."

Rigo turned to look at his parents then his grandmother. She looked worried. *She is afraid of me. She wants me to go.*

"Yes, I will go with you," Rigo said.

Alicia turned, sobbing in her mother's arms. Just as she had done as a small child when she lost her father.

The priests surrounded Rigo and turned to walk with him through the village. The path to the monastery was rough and winding. They needed to get back before dark.

The villagers gathered closer together as the sun fell behind the hills. They pointed at Rigo whispering, "Brujo" and "Shapeshifter" as the group hurried back through the village. The ridge of oddly course hair on Rigo's head and neck stood on end, bristling at the threats. He turned to issue a warning snarl, his jagged teeth dripping thick saliva as rocks and sticks landed around his feet.

The people screamed in terror, "El Chupacabra! El Chupacabra has returned!"

You Give Me Fever

Paul Edwards

It didn't take long to find her. Gossips in shabby pubs directed me to Nash House where a loose-tongued neighbour disclosed Mary's flat number. I thanked the neighbour, took the lift up to the second floor and drifted along a corridor to her pale, unpainted door.

Winter was loosening its grip on me – warmth and sensation spread through my frame as I rapped at the letterbox. I tugged my coat collar, suddenly feeling nauseous and out of breath. Without warning, the door jolted open and a security chain snapped taut.

"Please," I said, splaying out my hand against the door. "Please, Mary. I just want to talk."

A strangled cry came from within and I wondered if the shock might be enough to kill her. Then I took my hand away and the door slammed on me. "Mary? Mary … *please.*"

I stopped calling her after a while and tilted my head forward so that it rested against the door. I stood very still, breathing hard against wood. In my head I saw dirty creases in the air, black lines moving toward me. I smiled briefly, emptily to myself. Then the door jerked open and I seized the doorframe to avoid falling at her feet.

She'd gone back inside but had taken the chain off its hook. I shuffled forward, scuffing the soles of my shoes on a doormat. There were some wooden steps leading up to a room that was just out of sight. I took them carefully, the treads creaking and complaining beneath me, my hand gripping a loose rail as I ascended.

I edged into the sitting room just as the old woman was easing herself into an armchair next to the window. I caught a glimpse of myself in the glass and, as usual, convinced myself it was him looking in on things, appealing in vain for acceptance and companionship – a distant echo of my own pitiable existence in this world.

Her Gorgon stare fixed me and I quickly looked away, trying to seek a trace of the familiar within the room. Weirdly, I thought of the pornography Aiden had written about – stuff she used to make him watch – but there was none of that here. Perhaps it was stored in a drawer somewhere, or perhaps it was long gone, destroyed in a fit of panic when the authorities had pounced. I began to recall details of our house back in Digbeth. Paisley wallpaper. Tall windows shuttered against the sunlight. That splintered door beneath the stairs. The half-formed things in jars in the cellar...

"Well, this is a surprise," she said, interrupting my thoughts, squirming in her seat as I perched myself on the sofa. "Didn't think I'd see you again. Thought I'd found a place to escape everything. Guess I thought wrong." She rubbed her eye vigorously with a fist. "The date's not lost on me, you know. If I'd have known you were coming, I might've got something in. We could have had a celebration." She laughed mirthlessly at her words.

The air was thick and uncomfortably hot. A film of sweat broke out across my forehead. I thought about taking my coat off but I didn't want to forget it and leave it here. I wished I was outside, in the cold, anesthetised by winter once more.

"Why this year?" Her grey eyes glittered with distrust. "You want answers? Is that it?" Her expression mutated into a maniacal mask of contempt. "We breathed life into you, Martin. *Both* of you. But it was too much … especially for your father's wretched conscience." She laughed another humourless laugh, then waved her hand dismissively as she tugged her cardigan around her shoulders. "It wasn't that I preferred Aiden, of course. I just wasn't allowed to keep you both. Perhaps in hindsight I made the wrong decision, considering…" She pulled in a breath. "Still, you were given to a good home, right? Given to people who accepted you for what you are. Probably better off where…"

"I don't want answers." I shook my head, cutting her off mid-sentence, sweat flicking off my face. "This isn't about me."

"Then what is this about?" Her cheekbones twitched as she gripped the armrests and straightened in her chair, her wizened fragility disappearing before my eyes. "There's nothing for you here. There never was!"

I noticed a picture standing on top of the bookcase, one that wasn't grey and made up of flecks.

I got to my feet, snatched it up. He looked about fifteen, a shy, strained smile creasing his face.

There was more than a hint of sadness to that expression, I felt.

"After his father died, he was all I had." She nodded at it, her voice drained of emotion. "It was his madness, not mine. It always was."

I briefly closed my eyes, my heart hammering away inside of me.

I remember reading about the diary the detectives had found in his flat: a vicious, hate-filled thing that became more violent and rambling as it went on, frequently name-dropping Mary and all her terrible misdemeanours.

I opened my eyes, sighed, and stood the picture back up on the bookcase.

She was talking again but I wasn't listening anymore. I could smell formaldehyde and was opening the splintered door beneath the stairs…

I wished we'd stayed down there now. Wished we'd never been made to leave that womb of dust and darkness.

Above all else, I wished we'd never been separated, Aiden and I.

He was the only one who could have known what it's like to be me.

Mary's voice was raised now, her words betraying her madness; a madness that became Aiden's reality and filled him with a fever there could be no recovery from, no cure for…

"…not a child, no. More like a sick animal, a sick dog. And then he wanted us to make him a girl, a female companion; something to fuck, I suppose. He wasn't right in the head. We should have aborted before we even attempted to…" She shook her head viciously. "He was filled with such uncertainty and self-pity. Took after his father for that, I suppose. And the ironic thing was, they both went the same way – knotting their hospital bedding into nooses and then leaving me here to face a barrage of unwanted attention *all on my own*." Her wizened claws bunched into fists in her lap. "And the business with the whores ... those three women *he* butchered that night, validating my belief he was a mistake, that we should never have made him."

I sat down and stared at her wild-eyed form. Remembered the newspapers, the TV reports, the widespread horror and condemnation of him.

"...and he wrote it was *me*," she prodded at herself with a finger. "The *poison* of my body and mind, infecting *his* world. Couldn't he see I was trying to *protect* him? Toughening him up so he could grow into the man he *needed* to be?"

Spit exploded from her mouth as she gloated about having never been incriminated or sectioned, but I was tuning out of her paranoid diatribe.

Survival through denial. Mary was an adept.

I was burning up, sweat trickling down my brow to soak and sting my eyes. I glanced round and saw the radiator beside me, tapping it first with my knuckles before gripping it with my fingers. Cold. I breathed and saw vapour, yet my body was bathed in sweat.

I stared at Mary, clouds of mist escaping her lips as she glared at me with eyes of ice and fire, then allowed my gaze to slide across to the figure framed in the windowpane beside her. "It wasn't your fault," I whispered and offered him the scantest of smiles. "Not really."

I often think it should have been me. Not him.

And the guilt never goes away, no matter how often I try telling myself it hadn't been my fault, that I'd been too young and powerless to have ever been able to change anything.

I spoke then and the words which tumbled from my lips were distant and unreal, like when your sinuses are blocked and your own voice sounds like a ghost chattering in your ear: "I have a love in me that you can scarcely imagine."

I found my feet, disgust and panic exploding across her face as I approached her. I sank to my knees and opened my arms out wide.

"Hold me, Mother." That made her wince and I laughed, meekly. "It's all I've ever wanted."

She tried to bat me away but I wrapped my arms around her and pulled her in close. In a bid to connect to something, anything, I craned my head forward and focused on the mug beside her. My sullen reflection rippled on the surface of her tea, gaunt and feral-looking in the pale-brown liquid. Except it wasn't my face; it was *his* face, getting clearer and stronger all the time, like a photograph in developing fluid. And he was grinning, nodding his head with approval as I squeezed.

She began to squirm and thrash but I hugged her fiercer, tighter, enveloping her. My left hand gripped the wrist of my right arm, squeezing with all my might until I heard a bone crack and an animal sound escape her.

I kept hugging and twisting until the tears and the sweat streamed down my face and my eyes were filled with bright, hallucinatory patterns. I swallowed a scream and ground my teeth together, squeezing even harder. In time I let go and she sagged like a doll in my arms. My head felt as though it was on fire. I stood unsteadily, bumping into the wall as she slipped off her armchair to fall in a heap on the floor. She looked deformed and twisted on the carpet, like something she and Dad might have conceived in their make-shift laboratory before the police and Social Services intervened. I kicked her. She didn't move.

I turned, walked out the room and trudged downstairs with sweat dripping from my trembling body. I stumbled along the corridor and pushed through the communal door into the courtyard outside. The beads of sweat on my forehead joined and became trickling rivulets of coldness down my cheeks. I scurried out the main gates and kept walking without aim or purpose until I'd stopped perspiring and my heart had slowed to its normal rate. Soon winter's chill reached my bones and I was so desperately glad. I could see the cold again as dirty creases in the air, black lines moving toward me. Something flickered in the corner of my vision. I whirled, focused and beheld a shape twitching upon the surface of a shadowy shop window.

We were cut from the same cloth – we'd always looked similar – so it's easy to imagine he's here, still around, and I'm not alone in this world.

"Happy birthday."

134

The words left me in a plume of vapour. Our strained smiles slipped from our faces as the illusion of him began to fade. Then I turned and hurried on, into the anesthetising cold, eager not to feel anything but numb again.

Midnight Rider

Liam A. Spinage

"Listen my children and you shall hear!" The crowd hushed and shuffled closer as he began. "They say he rides out at midnight. The same night every year. The same night as his first fateful ride. Tonight."

Brett's voice was hushed, partially to keep up the mystique of his own storytelling and partially because he was carried away in the narrative himself. There was a small crowd gathered round him, hanging on his every word. At least, that's what he assumed. There was very little to see in the gloom of an overcast east coast evening, especially this far out of town. But he had takings for forty people in his back pocket (cash only, it was always cash only) so he figured he had forty people. In the distance to the north were a few flickering headlights and occasional traffic noises from the highway. To the east, the Boston skyline was illuminated by the suffused glow of light rain and the moonlight flowing overall. He hoped the signal system would still work as Amy said it would. They hadn't really had a chance to test it properly when they'd come up with this ghost walk shtick.

Too late to worry now. Brett was pretty confident he could wing it. It was his story, after all, and his carefree sing-song voice doing the telling. He warmed to the feel of the rapt crowd even as he huddled further in his greatcoat, the damp of the river fog clinging to his lanky frame. The crowd were the only thing warming him at the moment; later it would be good beer, good company and then just him and Amy.

"Shhhh." The crowd had picked up a little low chatter while Brett had been lost in his own thoughts. "Now look to the east. You can just make the city out through the rain - that's it over there. We have another member of the team on active standby. She'll warn us when the horseman is about to start out towards us. Look up, you'll see what I mean."

Brett fumbled in his coat pocket for his phone. Without removing it from his pocket, he pressed a single button to send a message, all the time with his eyes firmly on the shape of the crowd all craning their necks without knowing exactly why.

Putty in my hands.

***

Amy's phone buzzed angrily on the rail beside her, almost knocking itself to the floor and definitely waking her up. She rubbed her eyes to reacquaint herself with the near-darkness of the bell tower and suddenly remembered what she was there for as she saw the single word of Brett's text message.

NOW

Damn it, Brett, you're early. Couldn't you have kept them talking for just a little longer? She reached down through a tangle of cables to where

137

two powerful lamps were perched on the window sill and hit the ON switches. After that she reckoned she'd have about a minute before the lamps began to attract the attention of the authorities. If everything went to plan, by then they would have done their job and she could turn them off in time. If not... well she preferred not to think about that, but she did have a nearby bolthole just in case. She was a lot more prepared than Brett. She had to be really, because as cute as he was Brett was a dreamer, not a thinker.

She reached down and flicked the switch. There was a low hum as the lights began to power up, but apart from that there was only the secret dread of the lonely belfry.

***

The crowd let loose with a loud "Oooh!". Brett looked up with them and was surprised at the light he saw coming from the church.

Nice work, Amy! Wow, that really is atmospheric. He'd been worried that the lamps she'd borrowed from their roadie friend wouldn't be up to the task, but clearly she'd surpassed herself. Not only were they bright enough to breach the long distance from the city, she'd also managed to rig them with some muted blue-green filter which permeated through the rain and even penetrated the mist down here by the river, lending an extra layer of spookiness to the scene.

"The beacons are lit!" His cry cut through the murmurs of his audience and a ripple of silence passed over them. He lowered his own voice to meet it. "Follow me, if you please. That's right, slowly now, we don't want anyone slipping in the mud. Quietly, thank you, yes, let's keep the noise down as much as we can. We don't want to scare the ghost, after all." As they trudged forward, Brett fumbled once more for his cellphone and sent a second text to a different number. Irritatingly, he saw he'd missed a call from Amy, who was supposed to be maintaining radio silence. He briefly wondered if she was in any trouble, but decided to press on regardless. He'd find a way to call her quickly when the crowd were distracted by the sight of the midnight rider.

***

Jason swore under his breath as his phone buzzed. He'd been sitting here for nearly an hour now and in his boredom had taken to smoking a joint. Beside him, the horse he'd 'borrowed' from the Van Tassel stables whinnied softly. Whatever it was saying, it seemed to be about as impressed by the weather as he was. Stamping out his smoke on the damp ground, he checked the incoming message.

YOU'RE UP

Well, then. Time to freak out some unsuspecting rubes. He managed to mount the horse easily enough and set them into an easy but slow trot. The bioluminescent paint - also 'borrowed' - still covered parts of them both even though the perpetual light rain had washed some of it off. He hoped that what remained was enough, then remembered that Brett was paying him the same cut regardless and relaxed further, intent on enjoying himself whatever the weather.

As they clopped forward, however, Jason saw something which set them on a different path altogether.

***

The crowd shuffled forward, keeping to a low hush. Brett had allowed them to push forward without him, the lantern he'd hung at the edge of the little bridge clearly visible now and marking the point where they'd be able to spot Jason on the opposite bank. When they were all in front, he took out his cellphone again and, his face lit eerily by the screen, listened to whatever it was Amy had been so keen to tell him.

"Brett? Brett! Oh my god, Brett please pick up! That wasn't me! I don't know what the fu... Shit, there's someone coming. Brett, you there? Help! The lamps didn't work. I don't know what happened, but all of a sudden there were these other lights and...oh god, someone's knocking on the door, what should I do? Brett, pick up, please? Please! I'm so scared. There must be two or three of them right outside the door, I've got nowhere to go, my dad'll kill me, there's..."

There then followed an almighty crashing sound which Brett figured must be the door being broken down. The last thing he heard Amy call out before she was cut off was something about them

140

coming for her. After that everything went dead. It was at that point, down by the bridge, that the screaming began.

***

"Whoa! WHOA!"

The first of these exclamations was an instruction from Jason to his ignoble steed. The second was more of a panicked utterance as he tried desperately to get away. The air around him suddenly crackled with fearful energies which caused his horse to rear uncontrollably and snort in sheer terror. Then, seemingly from out of nowhere, the mist nearby coalesced into the spectral form of a man on a horse, which also reared as if in response to his own. Unlike Jason's horse, though, this spectral stallion appeared triumphant rather than terrified. As the man's head turned toward them, Jason saw straight through it to the woods beyond and decided that's where he'd rather be. Trying desperately to bring his own mount under control, Jason failed and then flailed as it threw him ignominiously to the ground as it raced off as fast as its legs could carry it. The last thing Jason remembered seeing before he passed out was a swift procession of twig, shrub and root as his head hit the ground with a thud. The last thing he heard was an echoing neigh as the rider urged his mount onwards to an unseen rendezvous, tricorn raised in his left hand as he held the reins in his right, and then the tramp of his steed as he rode forth. Behind and beyond that were the faint blares of trumpets, then only the pumping of his own heart and his frantic breaths, then nothing.

***

Brett panicked as he raced toward the ghost tour group. If he'd have known what was happening, if he'd have thought for a moment, he might have headed the other way. He might even have heeded his own advice about moving slowly so as not to fall over in the murk and the dark. Fat chance of that now. Half the crowd came hurtling toward him through the brush; the rest had scattered in other directions. Boots trampled, feet entangled, bodies fell to the ground. Brett himself was knocked over in the rush and by the time he had picked himself back up he was the only one remaining.

Except for the unexpected guest.

Unexpected was the right word. He'd never really believed the stories himself, beyond skimming the basis of the legend enough to run this scam. All he really knew was that the figure on the ghostly horse now gazing down at him was a most revered historical figure. He began to scramble backwards on his mud-stricken hands as full panic settled in. He was close enough to make out the horse's breath, distinct from the mist by its vague pale blue glow. He was close enough to see the whites of the rider's eyes as they narrowed on him and to hear his voice raised in anger.

"What manner of man are you, sir?"

Brett tried to raise a word in response, but nothing came out. He had given up trying to stand

142

now, but was still frantically trying to crawl backwards on only his hands and rear. He was not getting very far.

"I said, sir, who are you? To whom do you owe your loyalty?"

Brett faltered. "I...I, oh god please don't hurt me, let me go please. I'll give the money back. I didn't mean it! Just a harmless prank!" Brett was quick-witted enough to know that this wasn't what he needed or meant to say, but in fear his words betrayed his heart.

The rider paused for a moment. Brett looked around him. The fog in the whole of the little hollow the brook ran through had taken on a faint blue tinge now, like the horse's breath. He suddenly realised that the darkness was at once more and less intense than it had previously been and it took him a moment to understand why.

The two bright lanterns, - lit by someone other than Amy, apparently - were no longer there. Neither were any of the distant suffused lights of the city. That accounted for the darkness. Above him, though, the sky shone with the brilliance of more stars than he'd ever seen at once, accompanied by a full, gleaming moon.

What the fuck?

The rider looked down at him again, this time in pity more than fury. "I have no time for you, stranger. I must away, my task this night cannot be delayed. Pray they do not find you, whoever you may be."

Brett managed to blurt out one question quickly as the rider turned his horse around.

143

"Who do you mean by 'they?'"

The rider regarded him incredulously.

"The regulars, man! The regulars are coming!" This he spoke as his gallop began anew, fearless and fleet, even as Brett could hear the approach of hooves in pursuit behind him and spy a flash of red coats among the trees before he was overwhelmed by the experience and he lost consciousness, alone in the dark and the rain and fog.

***

"There's your share."

Amy, huddled into a deep blue hoodie, stretched forth a single freckled arm, pale and shaking. Framing her face through the depths of the cowl were locks of white hair. They had not been there before and Brett dared not ask just what she'd seen. Heaven knows he'd seen enough.

"It's not about the money, Brett." But she took it anyway. She hadn't asked Brett what had happened either. She'd barely made it back to the coffee shop herself in time after the church bells had woken her at midday. He didn't seem much affected, but she knew that not to be the case. She always knew with Brett. He'd taken a few knocks in his life, but he'd always managed to get back on his feet. She wasn't sure this time.

"Sure. I mean, it never is, right? Not really. It's about the thrill of the chase." He took the opportunity to smile, but it came out fake somehow. He averted his gaze from hers and stared out the window into the damp air of a Boston afternoon.

"Nobody contacted me. No reviews, nothing. You'd think, since I'd given them the real deal, they'd be a…"

"Cut it, Brett, I don't have time for this today. Whatever happened had best stay quiet, between us. Not that there's those who'd believe us. Not really."

Brett's eyes flashed alive for the first time since they'd met today. "Oh, sure they will. There will be plenty more. It's all in the telling of the story, you see?" He stood, wobbling slightly and coughed loudly for attention. The coffee shop patrons turned toward him.

"Listen, my children, and you shall hear!"

Amy sighed and took another sip of her coffee.

Sociopaths Wanted: All Positions Open

Diane Arrelle

SOCIOPATHS WANTED.

It started out so simply perfect, the answer to all my problems. And just in time. I was actually looking at the corner convenience store and hell, everyone knows they are always hit by unimaginative scumbags who can't chew gum and hold a gun at the same time.

Then, there it was, one day after their graduation. In the mail. An unmarked envelope with my name on it. I was going to throw it out because it had that bulk mail stamp and everyone knows that only junk mail comes cheapo rate. But something told me that this was important. Call it a hunch, and everyone knows hunches are important in my line. So, I fished it out of the recycling pile where I had tossed it and opened up the letter.

SOCIOPATHS WANTED.

I stared at that opening line for a few seconds my mouth hanging open like a broken ventriloquist's dummy.

SOCIOPATHS WANTED.

ALL POSITIONS OPEN.

Amazing, I thought. *Who could have sent this?* I read on, smiling at the joke. I would have suspected it was sent by a friend, but everyone knows I don't have any.

SOCIOPATHS WANTED.

ALL POSITIONS OPEN.

Tired of trying to fit in? Out of work? Recently released? Resent authority? Ever said you'd kill for some money? If any of these sentences describe you, call 1-800-KIL-LERS. This is the break you've been waiting for. At last, someone who really does understand you!

CALL TODAY.

The word sociopath buzzed through my brain, I like the words that buzz, that seem to tickle the inside of my head. A pleasant feeling. My shrink had used that term, sociopath, to my parents. Thank God they were always too busy to listen to anyone. They changed shrinks, five times. Mrs. Emery, my guidance councilor used that word too, right before they expelled me. And two weeks before graduation. Thinking about Mrs. Emery made my head buzz. She definitely tickled my brain. I smiled, no, actually, I grinned a big toothy grin. I liked thinking about Mrs. Emery. *See, Mrs. Emery, I do have feelings. Knowing you has made me very happy. Too bad about the accident.*

I really know I'm not a sociopath, everyone knows they don't have a conscience, that they have no feelings. But I do. I feel things. I like to feel things. I felt hatred for every teacher who ever misunderstood me, I felt a burning desire to repay every instructor that ever failed my work.

I feel so much that I know I am really an empath, I absorb other people's pain for them. I wish everyone a lot of pain so I can do my part for the world. Didn't I feel Timmy's pain after his dog ate the poisoned meat. Didn't I feel for the Donnelley family after their toddler mysteriously vanished from their backyard? Didn't I feel for the king and queen of the prom when the stage collapsed under them? Hey, I really do have feelings!

So, I called. Even if the shoe doesn't fit, you gotta wear it and I needed money. Thanks to not being understood, nobody wanted a genius drop-out. Since my chances for college were blown away, like poor Mr. Smith in the chem lab, I decided to control my own fate. After all, I'm the smartest person I know. Everyone knows that brains are the most important commodity a person can have. And since I've never been caught at anything they blamed me for, that proved I'm pretty damned smart, a fucking genius!

A man answered, "Yes?"

"Is this 1-800-Killers?"

"Depends," the voice said. "Are you seeking useful employment?"

"I'm seeking a job, man. I'm looking for a job that will pay me what I'm worth."

"Then this is the correct number."

A week later a black limo picked me up. Too bad no one was home to see it, too bad there was no one home to say good-bye to. But I knew that someday, they'd be home and then I'd come say good-bye. Yeah, I dream of the day when I'll come over for a proper farewell.

The limo had smoked windows, so all I could watch was the interior and the TV. The only channel showed carnage, body parts, murders, explosions, and I swear it all must be the real thing. I don't think actors can be that good at dying. Although the trip took a few hours, I wasn't bored in the least. I was riveted. I wondered if I could get this station on our satellite dish.

Then the limo stopped and the door opened. Two guys in gray suits were standing there. "Mr. Thomas Ames?"

"Nah," I answer feeling disappointment trickle down my windpipe and into my belly. I'm J--"

"Mr. Thomas Ames," the second gray guy said and stared at me with the coldest deadest eyes I'd ever seen.

"Yeah, Hi Guys, I'm...um...Thomas Ames."

"Come this way Mr. Ames," one of them said and they both about-faced and walked on ahead. So, I followed. We passed through two automatic black glass doors and entered a building as plain and gray as their clothes and hair. I followed, passing door after closed door until we came to the one we entered. We had turned so many corners I had no idea where in the building I was, but I figured that was the way they wanted it.

When I entered the room, there was another gray suit behind a desk with a file of papers that he has turned away from my line of view. "Mr. Ames, please be seated."

I sat and waited. Everyone knows the best way to act around guys in suits is to play it cool. "Mr. Ames, I've studied your background information and I must admit you are one cold-blooded bastard. You have caused a lot of people a lot of pain and grief."

I smirked at the guy, he was trying to scare me and I wasn't going to let it work. Nope not me. "Yeah? Well, you ain't got nothing, pal." I said. "The cops could never prove a thing."

He allowed himself a small, a very small, closed lip smile and opened the file. With an expert flip of the wrist he tossed an 8 by 10 full color glossy onto the desk in front of me. I looked and suddenly I didn't feel quite so confident. I stared at the photo of me standing over the body of that jailbait hitch hiker I had played with for a few days.

I felt like puking. How could they have this, how could they have known? He tossed another set of pictures, this time my hooking a bomb onto Brain Owens' corvette. The memory of the bastard blowing himself to hell felt good, like a warm security blanket, but knowing I'd been caught made my hands and legs start shaking. Looking into the gray suit's eyes, I felt very afraid. I opened my mouth to ask how they could have known, how they could have taken these shots when I'd always been so careful, but all that came out was a mouthful of vomit.

Those guys didn't even flinch. The main one just pressed the intercom and said, "Clean up."

I finished gagging and coughing and wished they'd offer me a drink or towel or something. But they didn't. They just watched me, silently.

"Ho... how'd you guys get these pictures," I sputtered pointing to the now soiled photographs.

Nobody had any proof... are you going to turn them over to the cops? I was scared, scared enough to pee myself. It was bad enough that there were pictures, but it was downright terrifying to think that someone had been around to take them, that someone had known to be around to take them, that someone had been watching me for a long time.

The one behind the desk finally spoke. "No one will ever connect you to those crimes. There is no proof in existence, as long as you cooperate with us."

Everyone knows you'd have to be an idiot to look a gift horse in the mouth, and I was no idiot. Even if I hadn't been such a friggen genius, I'd have known I was being offered a good thing. These guys appreciated my skill, I could tell. They knew I was a genius.

"Hey, that sounds fair." I said trying to appear dignified which wasn't easy covered with puke and piss. "Is this my job interview?"

The lead gray guy nodded negatively. "No, Thomas, these were your interview," he pointed to the smeared pictures. "Think of this as your indoctrination."

"So I'm hired?"

"In a sense, actually you are recruited. If you cooperate you can have an elite position with the Organization."

"Elite," I murmured knowing I sounded impressed. "Hey, I'm glad you guys found me."

They nodded and remained silent.

"But what am I going to do and just what is this organization, anyway?"

"Not an organization. We are The Organization. Think about all the paranoia out there about government conspiracies, cover-ups and assassin squads."

I nodded. "Yeah, I watch those stupid shows sometimes. Can't be real, politicians are too dumb to do anything that smart."

The gray suit to my left shook his head. "Yes, Thomas, it is all real and much much more. The Organization is the real government here. Only we in the Organization know of our existence, we only exist here and nowhere else."

I nodded. "You guys are secret."

"No, Thomas, we are more than secret. We are. And that is all you will ever need to know. We are and now you are... forever."

I nodded again. I could handle a lifetime job. And these bozos obviously handpicked me. I wondered when they discovered my talents, when they started watching?

And that was that. I became part of The Organization. Hear of any mysterious deaths? How about a big mouth neighborhood politician's sudden coronary, maybe that kidnapping of a newsmagazine's editor's child? Perhaps the population of a small town in the heartland somewhere coming down with some mysterious food poisoning. Maybe you're read about one of those flesh-eating virus's running uncontrolled through a country?

All I can say is, it's a good job with good benefits. I went through a thrilling training session.

There were six trainees, it was nice to be with my own kind. We were introduced to our trainer, a Mr. Larry Jones. Mr. Jones was given a three-day head start and as clever as he thought he was, he wasn't. I found him on day five and scored the kill. I even got extra points for cutting off his balls before I sliced him open. He didn't die pretty, kind of slow and fun to watch. I hoped they filmed it, because it was as good as any I saw in that film in the limo.

I was an operative for six years. Six good fulfilling years. It was a good job, good pay and incredible benefits. No matter what I did, they didn't seem to care. Just as long as I got the job done and I didn't make any mistakes. They didn't even mind when I did a few just for fun. You should have been to my high school reunion. So satisfying, oh the panic that virus caused. Everyone knows there are so many unknown germs lurking about. Everyone read about so many people needlessly dying. Warms the heart.

My life was finally perfect, I had money, women, job satisfaction, I had it all. Then one night the limo pulled up in front of my current home. Three gray suits woke me up, made me dress in my own suit and hustled me off to that gray stone and glass building that had become like a second home to me. I relaxed in the backseat, smoking a cigarette, bet you didn't know they have rendered tobacco harmless to humans. Not for the common folks to know, just another form of population control. As I dragged deep, I watched a murder on film, it took me a few minutes to realize that I was watching my last kill. A work of art, I slashed the

SOB as he sat in front of the tube. The fool in his desperation had grabbed at me, but I finished him with a final jab to the heart. Usually, I like to stay until they are done bleeding, until the last reflex has left their body, but I heard a car pull up and split. As I watched my retreating form, the camera zoomed in on the victim's hand, zoomed closer to his fingers, then closer to his nails. There was something under them. I put my hand to my head and suddenly realized where I had gotten that little scratch and I knew fear for the first time in my life. The Organization forgives greed, forgives double-crosses, forgives selling out. It forgives everything, except mistakes.

Just as the tape ended, we pulled up in front of the building.

"Let me talk to the boss," I said trying not to be forced from the limo. "Let me explain."

The gray suit nearest me shook his head. "No need to explain, Thomas. Mistakes happen."

This wasn't the answer I expected. Maybe they really do realize how valuable I've been to them. After all, how many guys are as good at what they do as I am? I started to relax. "All right," I said getting out. "Where are we going?"

The man smiled as he lit up his cigarette. "Your new assignment."

I knew these guys wouldn't throw away an operative as good as I was. "What's it going to be this time?" I asked.

"In here."

I entered a room with a mirrored wall and knew it was two way. Nothing unusual there. I looked

154

around and saw I was alone. I walked up to the mirror and waved at whoever was on the other side. Then I finger combed my hair and waited. Something about the setup was familiar but I couldn't place it. After what must have been an hour, a voice over a loudspeaker said, "Instructor Thomas Ames, you will be free to leave in fifteen minutes. Please leave immediately and give your students a full and total learning experience."

It hit me; The Organization was a job for life. I was no longer an operative, I'd become an instructor. Never let go, always employed in some capacity. "Wait." I gasped remembering why that room seemed so familiar. I had watched my instructor, the one I had so violently castrated all those years ago, gasp and stammer and flee.

I didn't want to beg, I remembered how I had laughed when he had begged, but I couldn't help myself. "Come on, I'm too good, too valuable to waste this way. I deserve another chance."

Silence, I was met by silence. "Don't do this to me!" I yelled just as the locked door snapped open. I looked around and realized I was dismissed, and that class was now in session. With tears burning my eyes, I tried one last plea, "Didn't I do everything for The Organization?"

The voice snapped out of the speaker. "Thomas Ames, you have your assignment. You were hired with all positions opened. You were given operative. Now you are transferred."

I went. And they are right, I have my assignment, to survive and beat those babyfaced sociopaths whoever they may be. If I get them first, perhaps I can get my old position back. After all, everyone knows I never liked teachers and I don't want to be one.

And most important, in The Organization, all positions are always open.

Meet the authors

Diane Arrelle has more than 350 short stories published and two short story collections: Just A Drop In The Cup and Seasons On The Dark Side. She, her sane husband and insane cat live on the edge of the New Jersey (USA) Pine Barrens (home of the Jersey Devil).
www.arrellewrites.com FaceBook: Diane Arrelle

Paul Edwards is a life-long horror fan and writes his own twisted tales in any spare time that he can grab. He has seen three collections of stories published – *Now That I've Lost You* (Screaming Dreams), *Black Mirrors* (Rainfall Books) and *Night Voices* (Demain Publishing), the latter being a joint-collection with author Frank Duffy. Paul is also a fan of role-playing games, rock music and rough Somerset cider.

Chris Marchant currently lives in the Normandy region of France with her partner and far too many cats. She writes mainly science fiction, fantasy and historical, but veers off course now and then. She is currently working on an historical Gamelit/LitRPG novel. Her website is www.chrismarchantwriter.com. She also has guardianship of #Drizztthemusecat.

Rickey Rivers Jr was born and raised in Alabama. He is a Best of the Net nominated writer and cancer survivor. His work has appeared in the JJ Outre Review, Stellium Literary Magazine, Fabula Argentea (among other publications).

Chris Rodriguez has retired from the horrors of conventional life. She now lives on the brink of inspiration in a 100-year-old cottage in Pocatello, Idaho. Her works have appeared in various themed anthologies including Rhetoric Askew, several by Horrified Press/Thirteen O'Clock, Left Hand Publisher's, *Mindscapes Unimagined*, ParABnormal Magazine, DL Russell's *Nobody Goes Out Anymore* and Blunder Woman Productions, *Wrong Turn,* which has recently won Best Audiobook Anthology at the SOVAS Awards. You can find her latest at https://www.chrisrodriguez-onthebrink.com or https://www.amazon.com/author/chrisrodriguez-onthebrink.

Rie Sheridan Rose multitasks. A lot. Her short stories appear in numerous anthologies, including Killing It Softly Vol. 1 & 2, Hides the Dark Tower, Dark Divinations and On Fire. She has authored twelve novels, six poetry chapbooks and lyrics for dozens of songs. She is also editor-in-chief for Mocha Memoirs Press and editor for the Thirteen O' Clock imprint of Horrified Press. She tweets as @RieSheridanRose.

E. S. Sibbald is a young writer working in the library and education industry. They remain alive only by devouring words and worlds. When not living in their own mind, they reside in Sydney, Australia. They can be found on twitter at @essibbald.

Liam A Spinage is a former philosophy student, former archaeology educator and former police clerk who spends most of his spare time on the beach gazing up at the sky and across the sea while his imagination runs riot.

SJ Townend hopes that her stories take the reader on a journey to often a dark place and only sometimes back again.

SJ won the Secret Attic short story contest (Spring 2020), has had fiction published with Sledgehammer Lit Mag, Hash Journal, Ghost Orchid Press, Bandit Fiction, Black Hare Press, Black Petals Horror Magazine, Ellipsis Zine, Gravely Unusual, Gravestone Press, Holy Flea, Horla Horror and was long listed for the Women on Writing non-fiction contest in 2020.

She has also written and self-published two dark mystery novels, both of which are available to purchase on Amazon: (Tabitha Fox Never Knocks, Twenty-Seven and the Unkindness of Crows).

Follow her on Twitter: @SJTownend

David Turnbull is a member of the Clockhouse London group of genre writers. He writes mainly short fiction and has had numerous short stories published in magazines and anthologies. His stories have previously been featured at Liars League London events and read at other live events such as Solstice Shorts and Virtual Futures. He was born in Scotland, but now lives in the Catford area of London. He can be found at www.tumsh.co.uk.